# PETTICOATS WEST

*Books by Olive Burt*

# PETTICOATS WEST

by

## OLIVE BURT

JULIAN MESSNER, INC.
NEW YORK

Published by Julian Messner, Inc.
8 West 40th Street, New York 18

Published simultaneously in Canada
by The Copp Clark Publishing Co. Limited

Printed in the United States of America

Library of Congress Catalog Card No. 63-16793

# 1 ‹‹‹‹‹‹‹‹‹‹‹‹‹‹‹‹‹‹‹‹‹‹‹‹‹‹‹‹‹‹‹‹‹‹‹‹‹

It was May in Boston. Abigail Cabot, stepping briskly along the path through the Common, paused a moment to savor to the full the beauty around her. Everything was vibrant with new life. The city seemed to exhale an incandescent green light as the clear rays of the sun struck into quivering animation the young leaves on elm and birch and beech tree. The emerald lawns and the grassy verges of the walks glowed with renewed vitality. Overhead the sky was a clear, delphinium blue, laced with fleecy clouds that raced before the brisk breeze that came, clean and salty, off the Atlantic.

With an impulsive gesture, Abbie flung wide her arms, as if to embrace the whole beautiful world. Then she smiled wryly at the pull of the too tight bodice across her firm young breasts. The brown merino had been made two years ago, and though the Widow Corey had let out the seams as far as possible, it was still difficult to hook up the bodice. Between fifteen and seventeen a girl needs more than a seam's width to accommodate her changing figure. Abbie dropped her arms and started on.

"Abbie! Abbie Cabot!"

Abigail's first impulse was to pretend she hadn't

heard. But there was no mistaking Sybil Wright's voice, even though she had not heard it for two years—two long and lonely years. She turned, waiting.

Sybil came up, breathless with running, her small, dark face vivid with excitement. She was about the same size as Abbie, but her nervous animation, her volubility, were in sharp contrast to Abbie's gentle steadfastness. In the past the two girls, arms about each other, had often gazed in a mirror and laughingly compared their looks: Abbie's curls were golden, her eyes gray and candid under straight dark brows. Sybil's braids were almost black; her dark eyes flashing. "Like as two peas in a pod!" they would say, hugging each other and laughing at their little joke.

"Abbie! Where have you been? I haven't seen you since—since—" she paused, flustered.

"Since Mamma's funeral," Abbie said quietly. "No—"

"I thought you left Boston—had gone to some of your relatives. But I kept expecting to get a letter. I didn't think you'd forget me; we've been such friends! Where have you been, Abbie?"

"I've been living with the Widow Corey, over the hill, near the hospital. You know she used to sew for us, and after the fire she took me in. I was sick for a while and when I got better I just didn't want to see any of my old friends. The fire took everything—Mamma, the house, all my clothes. I had to work to help pay Widow Corey for my keep and to get a few things."

"But me, Abbie! You shouldn't have avoided me! I've missed you so!"

Sybil's mother joined them, panting from the exertion

of catching up with her daughter. Abbie felt transported back to the happy days in the big house on Beacon Street. Mrs. Wright was wearing the same bonnet, its lavender ribbons in a neat bow under her generous chin, and the same gray shot-silk dress Abbie had so admired.

"Abbie, child!" she cried with warm affection. "Where on earth have you been keeping yourself? How are you? How are you getting along?"

"Very well, thank you, to both questions. Oh, it's so good to see you again! It's such a lovely day and now this. Somehow, all of a sudden, everything seems changed for me."

"She's been right here in Boston all the time, Mamma. Living with the Widow Corey, and keeping away from all her old friends. But that *has* changed, truly. We won't let go of you again." Sybil flung her arm about Abbie in the old, chummy way. "Where are you going now? Mamma and I are on our way to hear Mr. Asa Mercer. He was at our house last night. He brought letters from Hortense. Did you know she went out to Washington Territory with him last year? And Mamma and I are going with him this time. Hortense is married and wants us to come. She says it's absolutely wonderful country. Abbie, why don't you come with us to hear him? He's absolutely distracting!"

Abbie laughed. "Sybil, Sybil! You haven't changed a mite! You're the same old chatterbox. If you'd just give me a chance to say so—that is exactly where I am going— to hear Asa Mercer talk about Washington Territory. And yes, I did know that Hortense went out last year. I've read everything in the *Transcript* about Mr. Mercer and the girls he took out West last year. And when the paper said the other day that he was coming here to recruit part of a whole shipload to go back this spring— well, I just thought that maybe, maybe, there'd be a chance for me. The paper said he wanted war orphans and widows—and I surely qualify!" She smiled ruefully.

"So do we," Sybil said soberly. "Papa was killed at Kelly's Ford a year ago last November."

Abbie nodded. "I know. It was while I was still too sick to go any place. But I read about it. I was sad for you."

"But come, children!" Mrs. Wright interrupted. "We must hurry or we won't get seats. Look at the crowd of women already at the church!" She hurried on ahead.

"Let's not get separated," Sybil said. "I don't want to lose you ever again."

Abbie bobbed her head in agreement as the two girls gently pushed their way through the milling throng of women surging up the steps of the old Park Street Church.

"Do you imagine all these people are going to try to go West with Mr. Mercer?" Abbie asked.

"If they do, there won't be room on the ship for Mamma and me," Sybil said with a grin. "And he's promised to take us. We registered last night."

Inside the church Mrs. Wright had already found a seat and was saving a place for them. They crowded toward her and settled themselves. As Sybil fussily smoothed her full-skirted dress, Abbie saw with a shock that the ruching at her friend's wrist was frayed. Then she remembered that Mrs. Wright was wearing a familiar dress as well as the bonnet. So others had had a difficult time, too. She felt a prickle of shame for having selfishly hidden away, thinking her troubles worse than any one else's.

Still, Sybil had her mother, and her father had died fighting for his country. The old sense of futile loss engulfed Abbie. Her own father, as an army surgeon, had survived the dangers of frontier army posts with Indians, renegade white men, wild animals and a harsh environment. But he had died needlessly of food poisoning as the troopship carrying the First Massachusetts Volunteers lay in New York Harbor. Her mother had perished in their flaming home, alone, unable to escape, while her daughter was away at a school party, having a happy time.

A man was stepping into the pulpit, and the noise and confusion dwindled to a stop. Abbie sat forward on the bench. She studied Asa Mercer with interest. Ever since she had read about him last year when he had taken eleven girls back to Washington Territory she had been intrigued. The Boston *Transcript* had, from time to time, published letters from these girls, telling of their adventures, their observations, their successes in the wild country of the Pacific frontier.

To Abbie, helping the Widow Corey with the washing and ironing she did for a living, scrubbing floors, or "going out" when possible to do menial jobs for a few pennies, these letters had seemed a challenge. They beckoned to a new life that would be more interesting and more rewarding than her dull days as a hanger-on in the widow's crowded little cottage.

Now the man who was responsible for her dream was

there before her. He was tall and thin with rather stooped shoulders. His hair was carroty, and his bushy brows matched it in color. Under those brows, deep-set eyes seemed to burn with fervor. He wore an ordinary black suit, but Abbie could see that the material was cheap and the garments ill-fitting. She shrugged. What did that matter? It was the man inside the suit, no, the dream inside the man, that counted, and no one could doubt that this man was dedicated to a vision.

Mercer began to speak and Abbie started at the voice. Its nasal twang, the peculiarly enunciated syllables reminded her of the voices of the settlers around Fort Atkinson on the Upper Missouri, where she had spent two years with her father.

"My dear ladies," Mercer said, "your presence here indicates that you know my purpose in coming to Boston, as, indeed, you should, for my plan has received a good deal of notice in the public press, and from such prominent men as your governor and the noted Mr. Edward Everett Hale."

Sybil leaned close and whispered, "Isn't he utterly distracting?"

Abbie didn't find him "distracting," in fact she was disappointed. His appearance, his voice, the almost placating tone did not fit her preconceived notion of this "knight from the Far West." Only his eyes, burning in their deep sockets, struck the right note. Still, as she listened, she forgot her disillusionment and let herself get swept up in the romantic plan he was offering.

It was a logical project, as Abbie had long ago decided. Here in the East, Mercer pointed out, were thousands of widows and orphans, whose husbands or fathers had died in the Civil War. Moreover the manufacturing cities of the East were in the doldrums, starved because of the lack of raw materials from the South. With the surplus of females and the shortage of jobs, many were suffering acute privation and hardship.

At the same time, out in Washington Territory there was a tremendous surplus of men with scarcely any women to do the jobs for which they were "particularly fitted by nature."

"Seattle, Olympia—all the towns and villages are crying for teachers and nurses, for cooks and washerwomen and bakers and dressmakers. There is no end to the opportunities that await you out there!" Mercer declared.

He went on to picture the beauties of the country, the wooded hills, the sparkling streams, the fertile soil. The women listened spellbound to his description of this fabulous country he called "An Eden without Eves." He concluded by urging those who wished to go out to this paradise to sign up at once. He had been promised a surplus troopship, not needed now that the war was over. It could carry only five hundred passengers and he had come to Boston first, because of the fine character of its citizens—their culture and refinement. He was also going on to Lowell, New York, Baltimore and Washington, so, if any in the audience wished to undertake the venture, and could pledge the very reasonable fare of three hundred dollars, they would be wise to give him their names and assurances today.

A buzz of comment filled the room. A few women rose and made their way toward the front of the pulpit where

Asa Mercer was standing behind a table on which lay an open tablet.

"Three hundred dollars!" a woman next to Abbie exclaimed. "Land sakes alive! Where would I ever get three hundred dollars? I thought he was going to help us get out there, not make it impossible for folks like me to go!" She hustled her friend to her feet and they bustled out. Others were leaving, their disillusionment plainly voiced.

Abbie turned to Sybil. "Well, that's my situation to a T. Of course I can't pay any three hundred dollars, but then," she shrugged resignedly, "I didn't really expect to go. Only, the way the papers put it, I sort of thought—"

"Oh, Abbie!" Sybil cried. "Wait and talk to him. He is going to take some who can't pay in advance. He told us so last night. But he can't announce it, or he'd be swamped with those who can't pay. And even those who can, wouldn't want to, if some were going out on credit. Wait and talk to him, please."

Abbie hesitated. She looked toward the women swarming around the table, busily signing Mr. Mercer's book.

"How can all those women get that much money?" she asked wonderingly. "Haven't they suffered losses and hardships during the war like most of us?"

"Of course they have, that's why they're so anxious to get away from Boston. But I guess they'll find the money somehow. We're going to sell our house and furniture—everything we won't need out West. They must have things to sell, too."

"Yes," Abbie admitted, "I guess so. But I haven't anything."

Mrs. Wright rose, her gray shot-silk rustling importantly. "I was going to speak to Mr. Mercer, tell him what a fine address he gave. But there are so many around him, and he's coming to the house again, so we'd better go, Sybil."

"I want to wait, Mamma, and introduce Abbie to him. I'm going to ask him if he can't help her go out with us."

Mrs. Wright turned to Abbie. "You're serious about this, child? You've really thought it out? It wouldn't do to ask for help and then back out, you know."

"Oh, yes!" Abbie said. Her voice deepened with the intensity of her feeling. "Oh, yes, I've thought it out and talked it over with Mrs. Corey. I wouldn't back out. Ever since Mr. Mercer was here last year I've dreamed about it. And when the papers began to tell about his return, I made up my mind. I have been doing extra work and saving every penny—I wouldn't back out!" she repeated firmly.

"Then I'll stay, too. It may help if he knows that you will have the support and help of someone responsible, not just the enthusiasm of two fanciful girls." Mrs. Wright settled herself again with such purposefulness that Abbie had to smile as she thanked her.

The woman sitting next to Sybil's mother asked a question and Mrs. Wright turned to answer. They were soon involved in an animated conversation, with Mrs. Wright relating anecdotes about her daughter Hortense's experiences in Washington Territory. Abbie and Sybil chatted quietly about what had taken place in the two years of their separation. Gradually the church emptied.

"We'd better go and talk to Mr. Mercer now," Mrs. Wright suggested. "He'll be tired, I'm sure, and eager to get away."

The three of them made their way down the aisle. Abbie was eager to get a closer look at this man about whom she had read and thought so much. From the pulpit he had seemed more like a minister than an adventurer, and this impression was intensified as she drew near. His rusty black suit, his unworldly expression, his deep-set, burning eyes all bespoke the idealist. It disturbed Abbie a little. Her troubles had forced her to value a practical approach to life. Dreams were wonderful, and she had often indulged in them, but they did not get the daily tasks done.

"Ah, Mrs. Wright! Sybil!" Mercer greeted them as they came up. "I am pleased that you came today, even though you have already indicated that you are to be part of my flock."

"Yes. It was an inspiring talk, and I could see that many are eager to join you. I waited behind to have you meet Miss Abigail Cabot. She is a dear friend of my daughter's and a war orphan. She wants to go to Seattle with us."

"Ah, Miss Cabot! It will be pleasant for Miss Sybil to have a dear companion. If you will sign here, then—"

"No, sir!" Abbie said firmly. "I cannot sign, because I cannot pay my passage. I do want to go West, but I had understood from the papers that it might be possible for worthy women or girls to join your expedition even if they had nothing. I see that I was wrong—"

"No, Abbie," Mrs. Wright interrupted. "We told her

what you said last night about taking some passengers
on credit. If you can do this for anyone, you'll find none
more worthy, I'm sure, than Abbie."

"Ah, yes." He drawled out the "ah" and gnawed on
the corner of his lower lip, his shrewd eyes regarding
Abbie. "Ah, yes," he repeated. "It's like this, Miss Cabot.
If I can sign up my full quota of five hundred—or nearly
that number—who can pay in advance, I shall be able to
take on a few, a very few, who must wait until they
reach Seattle and obtain positions before they can pay
for the voyage. Ah!" he held up his hand to stop Abbie,
who was about to speak. "There are dozens, nay hun-
dreds of positions open. And there are many well-to-do
young bachelors who would be happy to pay for a ticket
for such a pretty young lady."

"Oh, no, sir!" Abbie protested. "I wouldn't think
of it!"

"There's no need to," he said reassuringly. "Mrs.
Wright, you'll vouch for her, of course. Then all she
need do is to let me take her name. I'm sure we can find
a place for her. And then she should do as I advised you
last night. She must prepare clothing for the voyage,
obtain some money for incidental expenses, and be
ready when I send word to come to New York." He
turned again to Abbie. "Can you manage all these things,
miss?"

Abbie was somewhat taken aback by the speed with
which it seemed that all obstacles had been swept away.
She gasped. "Oh, yes, indeed, sir! I'll work like everything! I'll be ready."

Sybil flung her arms about her friend and gave her a

hearty squeeze. "Abbie, Abbie! We'll have such fun! Oh, how lucky that I met you today."

"Yes," Abbie agreed soberly. "It was lucky. I'd never have tried to speak to Mr. Mercer, let alone sign up to go." Her hand was shaking as she wrote her name and age and the other required details in Asa Mercer's record book.

Mr. Mercer picked up the book when Abbie had finished. He studied what she had written, nodded, shut the book and stowed it away in a big carpetbag which, Abbie decided, must hold most of his possessions, it bulged so. He picked up his high-crowned hat and bowing low said to Mrs. Wright, "After you, madam."

So they left the church, Sybil's mother sailing ahead, Asa Mercer following. Abbie and Sybil, hugging each other in their happiness, brought up the rear.

Outside Abbie paused and lifted her face to the sky. "Oh, beautiful!" she breathed. "Sybil, I'm almost flabbergasted. Can it really be true?"

"It's true, all right. Now come home with me and I'll set you clear on the details—"

"I can't, Sybil. I must hurry back to the Widow Corey's. I must let her share my happiness and my hopes. She's been so good to me. And she sent me off this morning with such a cheerful word. I can't let her wait, but I'll come over tomorrow, sure!"

They walked through the Common, arm in arm. At the far corner they parted.

"Don't forget tomorrow," Sybil warned.

"Of course not!" Abbie said laughing. Then she turned

and hurried as fast as she could with propriety along Beacon Street and up over the hill.

Maggie Corey looked up from the ruffled shirt she was ironing as Abbie burst into the little room.

"You don't need to open your mouth, child," she said, beaming. "I can tell by that pretty face that you have good news."

Abbie flung her arms about the woman. "Maggie! Maggie! It does look as though I'll get to go. Oh, it's not positively certain, of course. But he says, Mr. Mercer says, that if he can get five hundred women and girls that can pay in advance, he'll be able to manage all right. Then he can take a few—a very few—who can't pay now. They'll pay after they get to Seattle and get jobs. Oh, if it only does happen to me!"

"I'm happy for you, child, though this cottage will be a dull place after you leave."

"I met Sybil Wright and her mother—I've told you about Sybil. They're going. Hortense, Sybil's sister, is getting married out there and is going to stay on— It'll be her home. So her mother and Sybil are going to sell their house and go, too. And they told Mr. Mercer they'd vouch for me. He doesn't want to take a lot of penniless people, of course. He has no money of his own, Sybil says, and he's got to have enough to feed us on the ship, besides maybe paying the government something for its use. He's serving the country—taking women out there to the frontier; so he ought to get the ship for nothing, and maybe he will. Oh, I do hope—Maggie, pray for it to happen!"

Maggie Corey brushed her hand across her eyes. It was a plump hand, but reddened and roughened from hours against a washboard. "That I will, child," she promised. "But don't go getting too het up about it. It'd break my heart to see you disappointed."

Ten-year-old Chrissie had listened wide-eyed to Abbie's excited talk. Now she came and put her arm about the girl's waist. "Don't go, Abbie! Please don't go!" she begged.

"Will you see bears, Abbie? And Indians?" her brother Jeffrey asked.

"Indians, surely, Jeff. And maybe bears. Shall I try to send you a bear claw?"

"Why do you want to leave us?" Chrissie asked tearfully.

Abbie stooped to the child. "It's not that I want to leave you, Chrissie. It's just that I must do something for myself. Your mamma has been good to me, but I'm a grown woman now, darling. I just can't let her take care of me forever."

"But you help."

"I've tried to help, but I must fend for myself now. And there's nothing much for me here in Boston. You'll understand when you get older, Chrissie."

She looked over the child's head into the widow's eyes and saw tears there. She couldn't stand it. She jumped up and ran to the room she shared with the widow and Chrissie. She flung herself across the bed and pressed her hands to her eyes, but no tears came. She was too excited, too happy, too full of the promise of a new life.

# 2 ‹‹‹‹‹‹‹‹‹‹‹‹‹‹‹‹‹‹‹‹‹‹‹‹‹‹‹‹‹‹‹‹‹‹‹‹

"MAGGIE! MAGGIE! IT'S COME! IT'S COME
at last!" Abbie cried excitedly as she flung open the cottage door, not waiting till she was inside the room. A
flurry of snow followed her, and she thrust the door shut
with an impatient push. Her curls, where they escaped
the warm, knitted hood, were white with snowflakes.
Her cheeks were rosy with the cold, her eyes shining like
winter stars.

"See, Maggie! Sybil let me take this letter to show
you." She held out a sheet of paper, her mittened hand
trembling with excitement. The woman glanced at the
letter, but didn't offer to take it. Suddenly Abbie remembered that Maggie Corey couldn't read and she
drew back her hand.

"It's from Mr. Mercer," she said more quietly. "He's
got a ship at last. We're to be in New York ready to sail
on the first of January. What a wonderful New Year's
gift! We'll be starting the new year and a new life on the
very same day. Isn't it marvelous?"

Maggie Corey sank into a chair. "I declare to goodness, child, I never dreamed it would happen. After all
these months! Are you certain sure there's no mistake
now?"

19

"Of course there's no mistake. It's all settled. He's arranged for the *Continental*." She looked again at the letter she held, though its information was burned into her mind. "He says it's a fine ship, much better than the one he had been promised. It's a shame he's had so many setbacks and disappointments, but somehow I knew he'd succeed at last. There was something in his eyes, a sort of fire, that I was sure no misfortune could quench. I know that Sybil became discouraged and so did some of the others. But not me!"

"That you didn't, child, but it frighted me to see you so sure. All these months—from May to December!" She clicked her tongue and shook her head as if the girl's steadfastness was an astonishing thing.

Abbie laughed. "I was really glad for the delay. It gave me more time to save up some money and collect a wardrobe, which I never could have done but for your fine scheming." She flung herself down beside the woman. "Maggie, I want you to know how grateful I am. I can never, never thank you. All those clothes—"

"Whoosh, child!" The widow's plump cheeks flushed with pleasure at the girl's words. "Twan't anything. Old clothes that weren't worth the charge I'd make to fix 'em up for their stylish owners. When I mentioned my price and suggested 'twould be better to just give them to you, they saw the sense in it."

Abbie chuckled. "You're a fraud, that's what you are! You just put on a big price so's they'd give them to me. I'm grateful to your customers, too, Maggie. But having all these months in which to get ready really helped me a lot."

She got to her feet. "I'll have to pack that little chest you wheedled from your beloved Father Casey for me. I hope it will hold everything. Imagine! Me with a chestful of clothes!"

" 'Tis a mighty small little chest, though," Maggie reminded her. "But don't be in such a hurry, child. There's plenty of time. When will you be leaving Boston, then?"

"On Thursday, Mrs. Wright said. We'll go down to New York on the night boat. We'll have one night in the city. Mr. Mercer says he's made arrangements for us to stay at the Merchants' Hotel." Her face and tone sobered. "The last time I stayed in a hotel was seven years ago, with Papa and Mamma. It was when we were coming to Boston, after Papa gave up his position as an army surgeon and decided to settle down. So long ago—before the war started." She brooded a moment over the past years and the changes they had brought. Then she shook off the feeling. "I mustn't stand here mooning. I'm sure I'll find plenty to keep me busy these next three days."

She took off her cape and hung it on its peg behind the door. As she drew off her mittens her eyes fell on her hands, once soft and white, now roughened by the work she had been doing at the hospital. "Slop work," Maggie called it, and that's just what it was! But it had paid her in cash, not much, but it was the only work she could find, what with so many women seeking employment at any wage. Abbie shrugged. She'd take along a jar of Maggie's mutton-tallow salve and in a few days on the ship her hands would be soft and white again.

Thursday morning dawned clear and bright and cold. Abbie and Maggie, Chrissie and Jeff were all agog with excitement.

"I'd better check that chest to be sure you haven't forgotten anything," Maggie said when the breakfast had been cleared away.

Abbie laughed. "How could I forget anything? All I own is in the chest. There's nothing left anywhere, I'm sure."

"You put the lavender-sprigged muslin that Sybil's aunt gave you down in the bottom? With the little black lace shawl and the summer petticoats? 'Twill be a long time before you'll be wanting those summer things."

"Yes, I packed just as you told me to," Abbie said, smiling. "Summer things at the bottom, winter things at the top. My pretty straw bonnet with the lace and pansies, and my velvet with the ostrich tips are well-stuffed to keep their shape, and in my bandbox. I'll want nothing but this warm knitted hood you made me while we're on the wintry sea."

Chrissie came forward shyly. "Here's something I made you, Abbie." She held out a long knitted scarf. "It will keep your neck warm."

Everything was done and ready, with impatient hours of waiting until Mrs. Wright and Sybil called for her. They had hired a van to take their chests and parcels to the wharf, and a carriage for themselves, and they were letting Abbie share both. The van came first, and Abbie's little chest and bandbox and a basket of food were hoisted onto the conveyance. The Coreys and Abbie stood huddled on the front step and watched the van disappear over the hill.

When the carriage came at dusk Abbie was ready and waiting, well wrapped up against the winter cold. The Coreys gathered around. The children clung passionately to her, as if to hold her back by sheer force. The widow was openly weeping and this set the children's tears gushing. Abbie embraced each one, kissed the wet cheeks and promised letters and bear claws, watchfulness over her possessions, care in speaking to strangers, and love that would never, never forget her dearest friends.

At last she climbed into the carriage, settled herself beside her friends, and heard the coachman shout to his horses. She looked back and waved until the carriage topped the hill and started down the long slope toward the wharf where the New York ship lay waiting.

As they left the carriage and hurried along the wharf, a bitterly cold wind swept in from the sea. Abbie shivered and drew her cape more closely about her. There was no one in sight; the wharf seemed deserted.

"Where is everybody?" she asked through lips stiff with the cold.

"I suppose those that have come are inside the waiting room. We're a little early." Mrs. Wright tried to sound reassuring, but her voice was troubled.

About a score of people sat huddled on the hard wooden benches in the big, cold room. In one corner a potbellied stove glowed redly, but it was too hot near the stove, and the warmth was dissipated into nothingness a little farther out. Abbie's glance went swiftly over the waiting people. Some were surely of Mercer's company: Mrs. Peterson with her three children, Abbie knew, had signed up for emigration to Washington Territory. She had sold her small sweetshop to get the money. And there was Kate Barlow and her mother.

The three newcomers made their way across the room to the Barlows.

"Well, you stuck it out, I see," Mrs. Wright began cheerfully.

Mrs. Barlow was angry. Her small green eyes flashed as she answered sharply, "Turncoats and fools they are that have believed those lying tales in the New York papers. I hope Mr. Mercer doesn't refund a cent of their deposit, though Amanda Kirk says she'll sue him for hers."

"Goodness," Abbie said, "how many are backing out?"

Sybil said slowly, "I don't think Mr. Mercer will have enough to make any refunds. The poor man has been kept out here eight months when he planned to stay only two. His expenses must have been awful. Oh, why did the New York and Baltimore papers have to stick their noses into his business?"

Mrs. Barlow yanked open her reticule and drew out a small sheaf of newspaper clippings. "You may well ask that, Sybil. Just look at these! Have you read them? Here's one headed 'Petticoats to the Far West.' Humph."

This amused Abbie. She smiled. "It's better than one I saw, 'Mercer's Maids for Miners.' But I thought the one in the New York *Times* was really fetching. 'Mercer's Belles.' It is quite romantic. Only I don't like people thinking our only purpose in going is to get husbands."

Kate Barlow sniffed. "Getting husbands is at least honorable. What I hate is the way they make it out that we are going to be—"

"Kate!" Her mother stopped her. Mrs. Wright shook her head, her eyes rueful. "I'm afraid those are the stories that frightened many who had signed up. I just hope the good man can get enough passengers to make his expedition pay for itself."

Abbie nodded silently. It meant more to her than to the others, for if Mercer did not have a full quota, or near it, she would be out of luck.

"But he must have!" she ejaculated suddenly. The others turned toward her. "I mean, Mr. Mercer must have a full quota of passengers or he would have told us. You know he would, Mrs. Wright." She couldn't explain to these others, but Sybil's mother understood and smiled agreement.

Mrs. Barlow went on as if there had been no interruption to her thought. "Well, I, for one, am eternally grateful to the man. Who else in this whole wide world has ever trusted me for a red cent? No! It's cash on the line every time. But not with Asa Mercer! I could only rake up enough for half our fare to Washington Territory. But does he say, 'Stay Home then'? No! He says, 'Come along, Mrs. Barlow, with your daughter, and pay the rest when you get to Seattle and get a job—or a husband!'" She snickered. "Like Kate, here, says, getting a husband is honorable. What chance does a widow have, anyway?"

Before the boat sailed a few other women and girls

arrived. They collected in little knots, feeling very self-righteous, discussing and condemning their weaker, more credulous, sisters who believed everything they read in the newspapers. Some of the more antagonistic papers had claimed that Asa Mercer was taking the women and girls out to the West Coast to staff the saloons and dance halls.

## SHALL WE PERMIT OUR YOUNG GIRLS TO BE SHIPPED TO THE DANCE HALLS OF SAN FRANCISCO?

That headline and the scurrilous story beneath it had stunned the Boston women. Mrs. Wright had been angry.

"Of course it's all lies! Hortense says that Mr. Mercer was President of Washington Territory's university. He's a very honorable, God-fearing man! How can papers print such trash?"

"Even if it is a lie," Amanda Kirk had pointed out, "a lot of folks will believe it. And if we go with him, we'll be branded, whether we deserve it or not. So I'm not going!"

Others had agreed with her. Looking at the little group in the waiting room and remembering the swarm of wildly enthusiastic women at the Park Street Church meeting, Abbie was aware for the first time how many must have decided against going.

During the night the wind that had whipped at them on the wharf blew into a gale. The ship, making its slow way down the coast, lurched and heaved; timbers creaked as if splitting apart. In order to save their money, most of the Boston group had not reserved berths, but were spending the night in the uncomfortable chairs in the large salon. They were seasick and terrified. They sat huddled over pails, retching and heaving, their faces green with nausea.

Abbie wasn't seasick, but she couldn't sleep. She found an unoccupied bench along one wall where she could stretch out. It was cold there, but she wrapped her cape around her, shut her eyes and forced her mind to dwell on the wonders of the city of Seattle, where, she had heard, never a snowstorm came to bedevil the happy people.

It was a sad, bedraggled group that disembarked at the New York pier that winter morning. They stood in a little knot, looking about them, not knowing what to do or where to go. A young man in a checked overcoat, a fur hat pulled low over his ears, stepped up to Mrs. Wright. He pulled off his hat and bowed politely.

"Mrs. Wright?" he inquired, and when she answered, he went on, "Ah, I was sure I could recognize you. Mr. Mercer described you so well. Madam, I am Roger Conant, a reporter for the New York *Times*. I've been assigned the pleasant task of accompanying Mr. Mercer's expedition to Seattle. This morning, Mr. Mercer, being unavoidably occupied elsewhere, asked me to meet you ladies and escort you to the Merchants' Hotel. It's not far from here and we can walk, but a van will pick up your luggage and bring it along."

"I'm glad someone's here," Mrs. Wright said with

relief. "We don't know where to go or what to do. Mr. Conant, let me present you to the others. First, my daughter Sybil and her friend, Abigail Cabot."

"I'm charmed," the young man said smiling and bowing. "My regard for Asa Mercer grows as I see the lovely ladies he has chosen for his pilgrimage."

Mrs. Wright soon acquainted the others with the reporter's name and his purpose in meeting them. Encouraged by this proof of Mercer's interest in their welfare, their spirits rose and they followed the young man along the dreary street, walled in by ugly wooden warehouses.

They had reached the hotel and were crowded into the parlor while a confused clerk tried to register their names and assign them to rooms. There were not nearly enough rooms or beds for such a throng, and the clerk was having trouble enough when Asa Mercer rushed in. His carroty hair lay in dank wisps across his forehead, his trousers were snow-soaked to the knee and he was shivering with the cold. Abbie saw that he was even thinner than he had been in the spring, his cheeks gaunt, his eyes more sunken in their deep sockets. But the dedicated flame in those eyes was still bright.

He stepped onto a chair and rapped for silence. When the chattering stilled, he spoke in his quick, nervous twang.

"My dear ladies, I am happy to welcome you here in New York. As I have informed you by letter, the *Continental* will sail tomorrow. Everyone is to be aboard by eleven o'clock." A murmur of satisfaction interrupted him. He waved his hand impatiently and went on. "But before anyone goes aboard I must explain the situation, which has altered somewhat from what you are anticipating."

The women looked at each other with alarm. Sybil clutched Abbie's arm. "If anything happens to keep us from sailing—" she began.

Abbie hushed her. "Nothing can happen, Sybil. Listen!"

Now Mercer began with nervous haste to sketch his troubles and disappointments in getting a ship. The government had not kept the promise made by an officer last spring to let him have a ship at a nominal fee. He had tried seeing everyone in authority and finally had been offered the *Continental*. But he must buy the ship, and the price was eighty thousand dollars.

Well, he had tried to raise the money, but had been unable to do so. Then, just when he was about to give up, a Mr. Holladay had come forth with the offer to purchase the ship and carry the passengers to the West Coast for Mercer.

"He agreed to conform to my plan—to carry five hundred women and girls around the Horn for three hundred dollars each. However," he held up his hand to keep their attention riveted, "however, when those libelous articles appeared in the newspapers, many of my proposed passengers canceled their reservations. With you ladies from Boston, I have now less than one hundred of my original party!"

What did this mean? Dismay and anger found voice in worried comments. Why hadn't he notified them of this before they left home?

"I have hoped, up to this very morning, that things would change for the better. But alas! In this I have been disappointed."

Mrs. Wright got to her feet. "Mr. Mercer," she said in a firm tone, "please tell us, straight out, what you're getting at. Is the voyage canceled? You said the ship would sail tomorrow and now you say—"

"Patience! Patience, my dear Mrs. Wright!" the man begged. He dashed the hair back from his forehead and went on to explain. Since he had not been able to produce the five hundred women agreed upon, Holladay considered his contract with Mercer canceled. He was still going to take the ship to the West Coast, but he would not reserve it for Mercer's party. He would get whatever passengers he could. And any promises Mercer had made were also canceled. No one, absolutely no one, would be taken on the promise to pay after arrival in Seattle. Every fare must be paid in advance.

The last announcement was greeted by irate howls. Abbie felt sorry for the man until the full impact of his words struck her. He was no longer in control of the ship. And he could not let her go without paying, as he had agreed. Then why hadn't he let her know? Why hadn't he told Mrs. Wright? What was she going to do now?

Mrs. Barlow was on her feet. "Why didn't you write and tell us!" she demanded. "Why did you let us come down here thinking your promises were good? You knew very well, Mr. Mercer, that I could pay only half the fare for me and my daughter. Now you want it all. I haven't got it, I tell you! I can't get it! What am I to do now?" She was half crying, half screaming.

Mrs. Wright spoke into the confusion. "There are times when none of us can control our lives—or keep our promises—in spite of our most earnest efforts. I think this is one of those times for Mr. Mercer. But I have every confidence that he has done his best. I know he trusts us, just as I would be willing to trust any member of this party, if I had the money. I am as helpless as he is, so I think I understand his humiliation now. If I could have sold my house for cash, I would have had plenty of money and I would gladly have helped others take advantage of this voyage. But as you all know, there's so very little cash in Boston. I had to take what I could get. It is too bad that some must be disappointed. It would have been better if they had known—"

"Mrs. Wright. Dear Mrs. Wright! I did do my best to let everyone know how things stood. I did send letters—" Mr. Mercer interrupted.

"I never received one!" Mrs. Barlow said. "And it's all right for you to stand up for him, Nellie Wright! You're going out with him, so you know it's to your advantage to stick up for everything he does. But for us it's been an expense and a trial. I want my money back!"

"You shall have it," Mercer promised. "I am not one to take money from a widow or an orphan!"

He stepped down from his chair and came toward Mrs. Wright. When he saw Abbie, surprise replaced the anxiety in his glance.

"Miss Cabot! Then you did find a way to finance your trip? I am very glad."

Abbie looked at him. "No, sir! Like Mrs. Barlow, I never got a letter telling me that I'd have to pay in advance. I came relying on your promise—"

"But I wrote to Mrs. Wright to inform you— Ah, what could have happened to those letters!"

Abbie stared at him. Had he written? There was no reason to doubt his word, for what good would it have done him to drag them all down here. Then again the mails were notoriously incompetent. Still, those were rationalizations— What about her? What did she do now?

Mercer turned to Mrs. Wright. "You did not get my letter? I can't tell you how sorry I am—"

Sybil turned to Abbie. Her eyes flooded with tears. "Oh, Abbie, Abbie! What will you do?"

Abbie's eyes weren't wet. Her chin was thrust out, her voice determined. "I will get to Seattle somehow," she said.

# 3 ◄◄◄◄◄◄◄◄◄◄◄◄◄◄◄◄◄◄◄◄◄◄◄◄◄◄◄◄◄◄◄◄◄

Up in their room Mrs. Wright put her arms around Abbie. "Cry if you want to, child. I'm sure you have cause enough. As I told Kate Barlow, you'll feel better for it."

Abbie's back stiffened. "I'm not going to cry. Tears will do me no good." She moved away and stood staring out of the dusty window at the bleak warehouses across the way.

"I believe there's a night boat to Boston," Mrs. Wright went on. "I'll have to find out when it leaves. I'm sure it will be safer than the train for a girl traveling alone. I must get you started back before we sail. I couldn't think of leaving you in this city alone."

"Oh, no!" Abbie cried. "You can't send me back to-night! After I've come all this way, not even to get a glimpse of the *Continental!* Not to see you and Sybil off! I couldn't bear it!"

Sybil's voice was shrill with protest. "Oh, Mamma, that would really be cruel! It's bad enough she has to go back, but not even to have one night in New York. That's simply awful!"

"Anyway," Abbie said more quietly, "Mrs. Barlow is

33

not going back yet. She's going to try to see Mr. Holladay in the morning. From what Mr. Mercer says, it won't
do her any good, and I could go back with her. It would
be better than traveling alone, wouldn't it?"

Mrs. Wright considered this a moment and then
nodded her head. "If Hazel Barlow will promise to look
after you, that will be best, I suppose."

As soon as Abbie could get Sybil alone she said, "I am
not going back to Boston with Mrs. Barlow, I am going
with you on the *Continental*. I'm going to stow away.
Don't ask me how, but that's what I'm going to do. I
may need your help. I can count on you, can't I?"

"Of course you can!" Sybil was indignant that her
friend had even asked such a silly question. "And it'll
serve that mean old Mr. Holladay right if you can sneak
a ride on his ship."

"I don't intend to go without paying. I'll pay as fast as
I can. But I suppose it will take me a long, long time,"
Abbie sighed. Then she went on purposefully. "Now,
my first problem is getting my baggage aboard. Mr.
Mercer said a van would pick everything up early tomorrow morning. How would it be if I put your name
and cabin number on my chest and bandbox? Then my
things would be taken on board and put in your cabin.
I'll just hope your mother doesn't notice them until after
the ship sails."

"Suppose your things do get aboard and you don't
manage to, what will we do then?" Sybil asked.

"In that case I bequeath all my belongings to you. If
I can't get to Washington Territory, I'll have to go back

to Boston and the same drudgery of the past two years. I won't have any need for nice things."

Sybil regarded her friend with a worried look. "You wouldn't do anything foolish?" she began.

Abbie smiled. "Of course not, silly! But you'll have to think up something to tell your mother if she notices my chest. Now, let's slip down to that little room by the parlor, where all the trunks and bags are stored, and get that part done."

There were still some women in the trunk room, labeling their baggage as Mercer had instructed, but no one paid any attention to the two girls. Abbie picked up a small bottle of black paint, which the hotel had provided, and quickly printed "Wright, Cabin 11" on her small, leather-bound chest and on the bandbox with her two precious bonnets. She must not carry anything at all, if she managed to get aboard the ship, for she would have to give no hint that she meant to stay. That much she had already figured out.

When they came downstairs the next morning, Asa Mercer was nowhere in sight, but as soon as breakfast was over, Roger Conant appeared. He went straight to Mrs. Wright, as if he acknowledged her the leader of the Boston party. He bowed low and smiled.

"I am again delegated to accompany you ladies to your ship," he explained. "Your luggage is safely away, so if you will permit me," he crooked his elbow and Mrs. Wright placed her hand on his arm, "we'll set out."

"I'm going along to see you onto the ship," Abbie said firmly.

Conant turned toward her. "I've heard your unhappy story, Miss Cabot, and that of these other disappointed ladies." He nodded toward Mrs. Barlow and Kate and five other passengers. "My job is to get interesting sidelights on this emigration," he went on, "so I hope you won't mind if I use your story to rouse some sympathy in my readers."

"I don't know—" Abbie began doubtfully, but the reporter wasn't listening. He had turned toward Sybil.

"You don't know how happy I am, Miss Wright," he said gallantly, "that you are not one of those who is turning back."

Sybil giggled and dimpled. "Are you going all the way to Seattle, Mr. Conant?"

"That's my assignment, and a pleasant one it is. Though I don't think my editor gave it to me with the idea I was going to enjoy it so much."

"How many of the women are actually going, after all that has been written and the change in fares and all?" Abbie asked.

"I went over the passenger list last night," Conant said. "There are about fifty of Mercer's emigrants. Mr. Holladay has managed to get another fifty passengers—some married couples and about a score of single men."

"Only fifty out of five hundred!" Abbie said indignantly. "I should think you reporters would be ashamed! It's because of your stories that so many refused to go."

Conant laughed good-naturedly. "Not to my stories, miss. I am in favor of Mr. Mercer's idea. And I like him, even though he does sort of get distracted over details. I'm sure he is honest and his sole purpose is to serve

Washington Territory, and through it, serve the nation."

They reached the *Continental* and at the foot of the gangway Abbie hesitated.

"Why don't you come aboard, Miss Cabot?" the reporter asked. "It's perfectly all right for visitors to go on deck. You can even tour the ship if you wish. There's plenty of time."

"Oh, do, Abbie" Sybil cried. Her eyes shone with mischief. This was just what they had hoped for.

"Well," Abbie agreed, hiding her own satisfaction.

The deck was noisy and crowded. Some of the passengers seemed to have brought all their relatives and friends to bid them Godspeed. Children pushed their way among the crowd, yelling at each other, climbing on the railing and shouting to people on the wharf.

Abbie whispered to Sybil, "Keep an eye out for Mr. Mercer. It will be easier if he doesn't see me."

Sybil seemed bubbling with laughter this morning. "Don't worry," she said merrily. "He's not likely to see you. Look, he's over there surrounded by girls. My, but they are stylish! Mr. Mercer seems very attentive to the one in the green pelisse. I wonder who she is."

Roger Conant glanced toward the chattering group. "That's Miss Annie Stephens of Baltimore. I interviewed her yesterday at Mr. Mercer's suggestion. But it's so cold here on deck," he went on. "Wouldn't you ladies like to tour the ship? I went over it with Mr. Mercer and can show you all the attractions."

They accepted gratefully, and he escorted them along the deck and down the companionway. He pushed open a door to show them a stateroom.

"Along both sides of the vessel are staterooms like this, large and airy. Each can accommodate from four to six persons. You can see they are well-furnished. There are several large bathing rooms, and a cabin all fitted up for the doctor." He paused before one door. "I can't go in here!" he said with a chuckle. "This large salon has been prepared for the exclusive use of Mr. Mercer's ladies. But you may enter and look around, while I wait here."

It was a large, comfortable lounge with sofas and easy chairs and a supply of books and magazines donated by publishers from New York and Philadelphia.

"How I envy you, Sybil! Weeks and months to spend in this pleasant room with all these books!" Abbie said, winking at her friend.

When they rejoined Conant they found him talking to another young man, disreputably dressed in baggy trousers, a knit jacket and a plaid cap.

"May I introduce Worth Barton," the reporter said easily. "He looks like a tramp but he is really a scholar. He's going out to Seattle to find coal—and make himself a fortune!"

Abbie's eyes went past the shabby clothing to a lean, dark face and a pair of brown eyes that twinkled with mischief as the newcomer acknowledged the introductions. His voice was cultivated, but it held an almost imperceptible lilt, as if he were secretly amused. Abbie liked him immediately, though that hidden amusement annoyed her.

At Mrs. Wright's invitation, Barton joined the group. They went along to another large cabin which had been turned into a sewing room. Several of the very newest sewing machines were securely fastened to the floor. Conant went to a door at one end of the room. He opened it to display a closet stacked with bolts of material.

"Our friend means to keep his ladies busy. He plans to have you make all this stuff up into shirts which he will sell when he gets to Seattle. And if you finish it all up you can go to work on knitting socks. Ah, but he's a clever fellow!" The reporter winked at Sybil. "Maybe, if you can't sew or knit, you'll have time to look at the sea with me"

As soon as Abbie had a chance she whispered to Sybil, "I've found my hiding place! That cupboard in the sewing room. There won't be any work this first day, and I can sleep on some of those bolts of cloth. It's ideal!"

"I'll sneak some food in to you," Sybil promised.

Just then a whistle blew shrilly and an officer shouted, "All ashore that's going ashore!" The deck became a madhouse of tears and farewells, embraces and parting advice. Abbie kissed Mrs. Wright and Sybil, repeated her promise to take good care of herself, and turned as if to make her way to the gangway.

As soon as she was out of sight in the crowd, she hurried to the companionway and down the stairs, hoping no one would notice her. She found the sewing room, pulled the door almost shut—and waited.

The noise overhead dwindled. A horn gave a short blast, the vessel throbbed and began to move. Abbie hugged herself in excitement. She was on her way, really on her way to the beckoning West.

She sank down into a chair. There was no need yet to hide. Everyone would be watching the shore, waving to friends, saying a last good-by to the familiar sights. She wished she could be among them. It was very still here in the sewing room. The creaking of the ship's timbers, the shuffling of feet overhead and the muted sounds of voices only emphasized the isolation in which she found herself.

She couldn't stand it. She got up and went to a porthole and looked out at the receding land. The rays of the westering sun struck the dust-filmed windows of the rickety warehouses along the waterfront, turning them into dull gold. Abbie watched for a few moments and then went to the closet. She busied herself making a comfortable "couch" of the bolts of material. She wished Sybil would come or that she had a book or something to do.

As the early winter twilight fell, the door opened softly and Sybil came on tiptoe, carrying a pot of hot tea and some biscuits.

"I bribed the galley boy to give me this food," she whispered. "I didn't want you to starve."

"But how did you get away? And has your mother noticed my chest?"

"I told her I felt sticky and was going to the bathing room to freshen up. As for your chest, I piled so many of our bundles and wraps and blankets on it that it is completely hidden. Eat this, Abbie, because I daren't stay long."

Abbie was famished and the hot beverage was welcome. She hastily consumed the scanty victuals, while Sybil whispered about the events that had taken place above-decks.

"That reporter, Roger Conant, and his friend have been very nice to me," she said, dimpling. "Only the friend kept saying how he wished you could have made the trip. He felt very badly that you didn't tell him about your problem."

"He must have been just talking," Abbie observed. "He wouldn't really care—"

After Sybil left, Abbie settled herself for a long, lonely night. She had no night shift with her, but did not like to sleep in her dress, which would certainly look the worse for such treatment. Since no one would see her, she decided to slip off the dress and sleep in her petticoats. She folded the garment neatly and climbed up onto her rather hard bunk.

It was not too uncomfortable and the gentle motion of the ship was soothing. She wondered vaguely why people got seasick. Then she tried to decide what she would say in the morning when she walked out to confront Asa Mercer. But she was tired, and her eyelids drooped.

She was startled awake by an angry exclamation and before she was fully aware of what was happening, a large, bony hand reached in and pulled her out of the closet and down onto the cold, bare boards of the deck. She looked up into the blue eyes of Asa Mercer, frosty no longer, but burning with anger. Suddenly conscious of her lack of attire, she reached back into the closet and drew a fold of calico about her.

"Miss Cabot!" Mercer was fairly spluttering, "what does this mean, miss? Stealing aboard this way? Did Mrs. Wright—"

"Oh, no, sir!" Abbie hastened to explain. "She doesn't know I am here."

"We'll see what the Captain has to say about this! Come along!" He began to propel her toward the door.

"Sir!" Abbie begged, "I am not dressed. I can't go like this!"

In his wrath he seemed not to hear. He was muttering distractedly, "The Captain! Ben Holladay! What will they say? For me to permit—though I never dreamed, of course, that a well-brought-up young lady, vouched for by Mrs. Wright—"

Abbie clung to the calico, and as she was hustled to the door the bolt of material fell to the floor and was dragged along behind her. Mercer did not notice this. He hurried her out of the room and along the passageway. At the companionway the bolt caught and Abbie's makeshift drapery was almost jerked from her hand. Then the drag on her fingers was released. She glanced back, and felt that she would die of chagrin and shame. Worth Barton had picked up the bolt and was climbing the stairs behind her, a broad grin on his handsome face.

Abbie clutched Mercer's arm. "Please, sir! Please, let me get dressed. I can't go on deck like this! I can't!"

But Mercer, muttering his own complaints, paid no attention. And how could she go back past that grinning fellow? Abbie swallowed hard, thrust out her chin, and stepped along as proudly as she could. She knew her cheeks were burning, but she hoped she looked at least a little bit regal.

It was all she could do to maintain this pose as they

went along the deck toward the Captain's quarters. Now Abbie noticed for the first time that it was well into the morning. The winter sun was bright, but cold, the deck like ice beneath her stockinged feet. But that wasn't the worst. All along the rail were little groups of passengers, who turned to stare and then to giggle as Abbie strode along, her head up, in a brave imitation of nonchalance.

Captain Winser was standing forward by the rail and Mercer propelled Abbie along toward him. Some of the onlookers followed, curious and eager. Abbie's cheeks burned, and she looked straight ahead, not daring to let her eyes rest on the amused faces around her.

When they reached the officer, Mercer cried out, "Look here, Captain! A stowaway! I swear to heaven I had no idea! You'll have to bear me out in this, sir! Ben Holladay—he'll demand her passage money and she hasn't any! What do you do, sir, with stowaways?"

Abbie forced her eyes to the Captain's face. It was stern and unsmiling, the brows drawn together in a frown. But under those fearsome brows gray eyes were twinkling irrepressibly.

"Well, now," he said slowly, "I generally set them to work shoveling coal or swabbing decks. But then I've never had such a pretty stowaway as this. Why did you do it, miss?"

"Abbie!" Mrs. Wright cried, thrusting her way through the gathering crowd. "Child! Child! What happened? Didn't you manage to get ashore yesterday?"

An immediate hubbub rose around Abbie. She stood there, the center of it all, her cheeks burning. She was ashamedly aware of petticoat and chemise, only partially covered by the gaudy material she was clinging to. She forced herself to speak above the confusion.

"Captain Winser! I deliberately stowed away on your ship. I must get to Seattle. But Mr. Mercer need not be afraid for his fare. I intend to pay him just as soon as I can. I'll get work and turn every penny over to him—"

"But that won't do!" Mercer wailed. "Ben Holladay will want your fare when we reach San Francisco—and I have no money to pay him for you! I owe more now than I can ever pay!"

Roger Conant broke in, "I say, Mercer! If you already owe so much, what difference can her three hundred dollars make?"

"My dear! My dear!" Mrs. Wright was murmuring. "If I only could—"

Worth Barton stepped forward. "If you're afraid to trust Miss Cabot, I am not. I will gladly lend her the money—"

Abbie shook her head. "That's very generous of you, sir. But I couldn't think of borrowing from a total stranger—"

"That's right, sir!" Mrs. Wright said firmly. "It is better for her to owe Mr. Mercer—"

"What if several of us put up the money?" Roger Conant suggested. "Would that do, ma'am?"

"No!" Abbie repeated more strongly. "Mr. Mercer had assured me I could go and pay later. I must hold him to that promise, since he did not notify me of the changed arrangements. I'll sign a note, and I will pay it off myself."

And so, after more discussion and demurring and insisting, the interested parties withdrew to the Captain's quarters, the note was drawn up and signed, and Abbie was free to return to the sewing salon and retrieve her clothes.

Sybil went with her. In the privacy of that room, Sybil flung her arms about her friend.

"Oh, Abbie! I know how you must have felt—"

Abbie sank into a chair and covered her burning cheeks with her hands. "I nearly died!" She sat thus for a moment. Then her hands dropped and she looked up, giggling. "I'd never go through it again for a million dollars! But this time it was worth it! I am on my way!"

# 4 ‹‹‹‹‹‹‹‹‹‹‹‹‹‹‹‹‹‹‹‹‹‹‹‹‹‹‹‹‹‹‹‹‹‹‹‹

THE NEXT FEW DAYS WERE DIFFICULT FOR
Abbie. She could not help thinking that some of the
passengers regarded her as an interloper; she was sure
they felt that she never intended to pay for her passage.
But for the most part her fellow voyagers seemed to
consider that she was justified in stowing away. Many
of the young men seemed to admire Abbie's determina-
tion and resourcefulness. They greeted her with smiles
and welcomed her into every game or activity. Only
Annie Stephens openly showed resentment of Abbie's
presence by scowling looks and snide remarks whenever
Abbie passed by.

"Don't let her worry you," Worth Barton said, laughing. "She's set her cap for Asa Mercer; that's plain. And
she evidently thinks she is showing a proper concern
over his affairs."

As the days passed, even this slight antagonism faded,
as Abbie's genuine good nature and cordiality melted
any feeling against her. Mercer had called a meeting of
his passengers and outlined the rules to be observed:
They would be held responsible for keeping their cabins
neat and clean; they must all be prompt at meals; there

would be no labor on Sunday; each girl and woman was expected to make so many men's shirts each week; and there was to be no flirting between the unmarried girls and the ship's officers or Holladay's passengers.

Roger Conant and Worth Barton, as well as the first and second mates, blithely ignored these injunctions and at every opportunity they strolled the decks with the pretty passengers, or chose them for partners in dancing, charades or other games.

"Mercer can't object!" Worth told Abbie as they stood by the rail one moonlit night, watching the trail of phosphorescence that followed the ship. "He's flirting with Miss Stephens, as everyone knows."

Abbie smiled. "If you can call his sedate manner flirting! But," she gazed archly up into the handsome face, "is that what you and Rod are doing—flirting just to annoy Mr. Mercer?"

"You know better!" Worth began seriously. Then the old teasing note crept back into his voice. "We may be flirting, but annoying Mr. Mercer is not our purpose. It's far more sinister than that!" Then, "How's the shirt-making? Are you still the champeen—as Mrs. Peterson says?"

Abbie laughed. "My two years with Widow Corey made me a very accomplished seamstress! I really can do more than most of the girls."

"And Sybil says you do much of her share, too."

"Sybil's never had my experience. I'm glad to help her. Then we both have more time to enjoy the voyage."

As the ship sailed south the air grew warmer, the passengers more relaxed. The decks were constantly alive with the laughter and chatter of "Mercer's Hundred," as they now called themselves as distinct from Holladay's passengers. The children romped among the coiled ropes and climbed on the capstans, shouting noisily. The babies gurgled happily, or yelled lustily, according to the way they felt at any particular moment. The men organized horseshoe games and quoits. Gradually the demarcation between the two sets of passengers dissolved.

Miss Ida May Barlow, a music teacher from New York City, had insisted on bringing along her piano. It was placed in the large salon and battened down securely. Around it nearly every evening, a group gathered to sing. Abbie had a knack at rhyming, and she and Worth would bend their heads together over a sheet of paper while they composed jingles that set off gales of hilarious laughter.

Early in February the *Continental* crossed the equator, and, of course, there had to be a celebration. In vain did Mercer order that there should be no horseplay, nothing undignified. Among Holladay's passengers was Dr. Lorimer, fat and jolly, and always ready for a practical joke. He was chosen to play the part of Father Neptune. He dressed up in wig and beard of raveled rope, filched from the ship's supply room.

It was an open secret that Asa Mercer himself was the one to be initiated by a good ducking, despite the fact that he had crossed the equator several times on his voyages to and from Seattle. However, when the time came, Mercer could not be found. So, lacking their intended victim, the men ducked Old Neptune, himself.

At Rio de Janeiro the *Continental* lay by for a few

days. Roger and Worth wangled a picnic basket from the cook and, chaperoned by Mrs. Wright, they escorted Abbie and Sybil ashore. They ate their lunch on the grassy slope of a hill, overlooking the crescent bay with its silvery sands. Sybil and Roger strolled away to gather sea shells, and Mrs. Wright dozed comfortably nearby.

"Let's just stay here forever and ever," Worth observed dreamily, as he lay stretched out on the grass.

Abbie looked at him and could scarcely keep her hands from straying to straighten the brown locks, ruffled by the sea breeze. He reached up and took her fingers in his hand. "What do you say, sweetheart?"

It was the first time he had been so bold, and Abbie's heart skipped a beat. But she shook her head decidedly.

"I can't give up Seattle! Not after standing before everyone in my petticoat—to my everlasting shame!" But her eyes were dreamy. It was a tempting thought.

Worth sat up and drew her close to him. "We don't need to give up Seattle, then. Any place will be heaven if you will be with me. Oh, Abbie, my sweet! You know I love you. Will you marry me, darling?"

Abbie's voice was troubled. "You know I can't, Worth! I am not free to marry anyone. And—" She looked into his eyes and thought she saw mischief dancing there. "You're just teasing—or it's this romantic spot that's got into you. Come!" she stood up. "Let's gather some shells, too."

Worth stood up and took her in his arms. He laid his cheek against her hair. "I love you, Abbie," he said simply. "I'm willing to wait till your heart won't let you say no!"

He let her go and they walked slowly down to the beach.

The passage through the Straits of Magellan proved to be the most disagreeable and dangerous part of the entire voyage, but they won through, after a whole week of storm-tossed effort, and swung up the western coast of South America.

On a lovely, sparkling April morning the *Continental* steamed through the Golden Gate and into San Francisco Harbor. Abbie and Worth Barton stood together at the rail, gazing at the scene before them. It was a moving panorama—a new, raw town, its wooden buildings seemingly flung down any which way along the narrow, crooked, muddy streets. And around the town stood the rim of hills of breath-taking green.

"Look at it, Worth! San Francisco!" Abbie cried, flinging her hand out toward the town. "Oh, I've heard so much about it! And I've dreamed of it, but never really thought I would actually see it some day!"

Worth smiled down at her, his dark eyes full of affection. "Don't tell me that, Abbie, my dear! You knew you'd see it! And I knew nothing could keep you from it, with that determined little chin of yours. Ah, I'll never forget how stubborn and yet chagrined you looked when Asa Mercer found you hiding in the sewing room closet. A stowaway! I couldn't help laughing—"

"And I'll never forgive you for that, Worth Barton! Oh, I was miserable that morning. I'd planned to walk out, chin up, eyes flashing and proclaim myself an unpaid passenger. But he stole my thunder. I never expected him to come snooping and find me there. I was so embarrassed!"

"If he'd happened along earlier, before the pilot had gone back, you'd have been tossed into the tug and sent packing back to New York City. As it was, there was nothing he could do."

"He was really angry," Abbie said with a rueful smile. "I didn't think he'd get so upset—"

"That red hair of his should have warned you!" her companion said. "Yes, he was mad."

"But I'll pay him," Abbie declared. "He needn't worry. I'm not one to be beholden to others!"

Worth put his forefinger on the jutting chin. "Down! Down, little chin!" he said gently. "No need to be uppity." Then, more softly, "Abbie, don't you know how very hard it is for a little girl to stand alone in a man's world? Learn to lean a little. It will be so much easier!"

"I'm not a little girl, Worth! I'm a woman, turned eighteen, as you very well know since you—" She flushed and stopped. Much to her chagrin and everyone else's amusement, he had given her eighteen "pats" at her birthday party. "I've already leaned too long on others. Now I stand on my own two feet."

She turned away from the tender look in his eyes. "I do wish we could go ashore right away! Why does Mercer have to forbid it and keep us here, virtual prisoners!"

"He has to see Mr. Holladay, I suppose," Worth said.

It was nearly noon before Mercer reappeared on deck. By this time a great crowd had assembled on the dock. Sybil and Roger Conant joined Abbie and Worth where they stood waiting for permission to land.

"Look!" Sybil said, "a welcoming committee. Let's hurry down and be welcomed!"

Laughing, the quartet moved along toward the gangway, which was just then being lowered. On the way they picked up Mrs. Wright. But as they reached the head of the gangway they were stopped by Asa Mercer, who was trying to get everyone's attention.

"Listen! Listen, everybody!" he cried again and again. At last the excited chattering of the eager passengers quieted enough so that he could be heard.

"As I have already explained to you, we leave the *Continental* here. Mr. Holladay refuses to let her go on to Seattle. So we must remain here until I can find a way to get you all to that city."

A murmur of anticipation interupted him. Looking at the faces around her, Abbie could see that all were as eager as she to visit this fabulous city.

"This is a wicked city!" Mercer went on vehemently. "The most insulting thing ever said about me—and there have been plenty!—was that I would bring virtuous females to this den of iniquity. Still, circumstances have forced me to stop over here for a few days. I don't care what the other passengers do, but the ladies of my party are still under my care. I want you all to stay together; stay close to me. We'll go ashore and I'll take you all to a respectable hotel where we can put up for a few days. Please, ladies! Please do not cause me extra trouble. I am responsible for your safety, but I cannot protect you if you stray."

"Oh!" Sybil moaned. "I did so want to see all the famous sights—the Barbary Coast—"

"Hush, Sybil!" her mother said reprovingly. "We'll do exactly what Mr. Mercer says!"

"And you have two strong male escorts," Worth reminded them, laughingly. "Perhaps you'll appreciate us if you get permission from his nibs to let you walk out at all."

The passengers hurried down the gangway. As their feet touched the dock, a group of women who had been watching them crowded close.

"My dear, dear ladies!" one of the older women exclaimed. "We are here to rescue you! Oh, you poor dears! How fortunate that we have learned about your impending fate in time to save you. Come with us! Come away immediately! We have made arrangements for your care, and your baggage will be brought to you—"

Abbie and Sybil stared at the women. Mrs. Wright spoke up. "I'm afraid you have made a mistake, madam. We are stopping here but a few days. Our luggage will be cared for by Mr. Mercer—"

"Mercer!" a younger woman snorted. "That whited sepulcher! We are determined to snatch you from his clutches!"

The truth dawned upon all the young people at the same moment, and they burst into laughter.

"They've read some of those New York stories!" Roger said, chuckling. He took Sybil's arm in a firm grasp. "Aha! my beauty!" he said with an exaggerated leer, "you are in my clutches!"

"Let go of her, you wretch!" the older woman cried. She raised her parasol like a club and came at Roger.

Other women grabbed Sybil and Abbie and started to pull them away.

"Why, these women are insane!" Mrs. Wright cried. "They must be insane!"

"It is you who are mad!" the older woman yelled. "Mad to permit yourselves to be duped into the dens of this city. We have evils enough, heaven knows, but kidnaping women and orphans is not one of them. San Francisco will not tolerate this crime!"

"It's got past a joke!" Worth said angrily. "Come on, let's get out of this." He brushed past the women with their threatening parasols. Mercer came pushing through the crowd.

"Follow me, ladies!" he shouted. "Follow me!" He started up the street toward the larger buildings in the main part of the scraggly town. The rescuing women turned on him, belaboring him with parasols, calling him all sorts of vile names. Mercer ducked, and with his arms up to protect his head, raced ahead. Laughing now, the passengers from the *Continental* followed.

That afternoon Mercer called one of his meetings for his entire party. He laid down strict rules to be observed during their layover in San Francisco. The females would be permitted to walk out into the city only during daylight hours and only when accompanied by a male escort. They must be back in the hotel before dark. None of his Petticoat Brigade would be permitted, escort or no escort, on the streets after dark, nor under any conditions were they to enter a saloon or dance hall. Sybil pulled a faced, but her mother nodded approvingly.

"Mr. Mercer is quite right!" she declared. "And I

doubt that we'll be safe, even in the daylight, after that demonstration on the dock this morning!"

So, while Mercer frantically sought money and ships to carry his ladies to Seattle, the girls went sight-seeing and shopping in bevies, escorted by their amused male companions.

It was somewhat of an adventure getting away from the hotel, which was picketed by relays of militant women determined to rescue the poor, deluded easterners from the hands of Asa Mercer. Annie Stephens became hysterical over the insults cast on the agent's name and purpose, but to the others it became something of a joke. Abbie and Worth even went so far as to compose a lively song about the situation, which they sang joyfully as they ran the gauntlet each day.

Abbie came into the hotel parlor one day to find Asa Mercer bent over a table as if in pain. His long, bony fingers raked his red hair in agony. Annie Stephens was leaning over him. Thinking that he was ill, Abbie ran toward him.

"What's wrong?" she asked anxiously.

"Everything!" Annie answered bitterly. "No one will lend Asa a cent! Everywhere he goes they make fun of him and of us. He can't get ships to carry us on to Seattle, and every day we stay here is costing him more and more. He's lost so much already!" She began to weep.

Worth Barton, who had been unnoticed by Abbie, dropped the newspaper he was reading and rose from his chair. He came forward and asked pleasantly, "Have you tried everything, Mercer? What about selling your cargo here, instead of taking it on to Seattle? I heard you had to unload it and store it here."

Mercer dropped his hands and stared at the young man. "Ah," he groaned, "that's all you know about it. I invested my last cent and much borrowed money in those plows and shovels, the lamps and brooms and lanterns and rubber. I was taking these supplies to Seattle because they're needed there. I despise this city! Why should I allow these awful people to benefit while my own good friends suffer?"

Worth shrugged. "It was merely a suggestion. I don't think you'll make more on the cargo in Washington Territory. These people have money—"

"There you go!" Mercer cried. "You, who have known me all these months now libel me by suggesting that I am holding onto this stuff in the hope of getting a better profit! Ah! It's not the money! I want to help my beautiful region. I don't want to help this—this—" he stammered to a stop.

Abbie started to say something soothing, but the distraught man interrupted, "Ah, Miss Cabot, you had better say nothing. Ben Holladay insists that I pay cash for your fare—another thorn! Another thorn! I don't know where I'll get the money!"

Abbie flushed painfully at this reminder of her indebtedness. It was not the first time that Mercer or his special friend, Annie Stephens, had alluded to this.

"You have my note, sir! You know I can't pay you now, and you know that I worked hard all during the voyage. I made twice as many shirts as anyone else. I—"

"Actually, Mercer," Worth put in, "if you'd paid her a decent wage for her hours of sewing, she'd not be far in your debt now."

"Her work was voluntary—as was that of all the others! She was glad to have something to do to pass those long, empty days."

"Yes," Abbie admitted, "that is true. I was glad to help out. But those shirts—"

"Sell them here!" Worth said firmly. "And all your cargo. You'll realize enough to fulfill your bargain and get these ladies to Seattle." He took Abbie's arm. "Come along, my dear. Let's give him time to think things over. He'll see that he can do nothing else."

Much as he hated to let the wild San Franciscans benefit from his foresight in filling the hold of the *Continental* with needed tools and supplies Mercer finally came around to Worth's point of view. He advertised an auction of his goods, and was almost swamped by the eager throng that came to buy. He realized a handsome profit, and with that cash was able to pay for accommodations for his party from San Francisco to Puget Sound.

Most of Holladay's passengers had decided to remain in the Bay City, where everything was booming. Some of Mercer's party also chose to remain here. At the end of that hectic week, the rest of the female emigrants were divided into three groups and shepherded onto sloops which would carry them to their destination.

Abbie and Sybil were delighted when they found that Worth and Roger had managed to obtain berths on the *Maria,* to which they had been assigned.

"We won't have as good times on this little vessel as

we had on the ship!" Sybil said, "what with the parties and games and singing around the piano. But then, we won't have such a long trip to fill up with activity!"

"And we won't have any shirts to sew or socks to knit!" Abbie added. "Every yard of cloth, every skein of yarn went in that auction!"

# 5

<<<<<<<<<<<<<<<<<<<<<<<<<<<<<<<<<<<<<<<<

It was May again, just a year since Abbie had attended the meeting in the Park Street Church in Boston. The little flotilla sailed northward with everyone in high spirits. Even Asa Mercer seemed to have forgotten the nine months of disappointment and hardship and the tedious three months of the voyage. Exhilaration bubbled as the sloops entered Puget Sound, en route to Seattle. The long journey was ended.

Abbie gazed enchanted at Mercer's "Inland Sea." The shores were entirely covered with immense pine forests that climbed from golden beaches up the encircling hills to stand in dark ranks against the azure sky. Here and there, at the water's edge, was a small clearing where a few log cabins nestled. Over all lay a sweet and comforting peace.

"It's lovelier than Mr. Mercer described it!" Abbie said. "A true frontier! A virgin land! Oh, Sybil, here we can really prove our worth—shape our lives as we wish. Already I feel as if I am as new and strong as this wonderful land—as if I had been reborn."

"Well, I do hope Seattle is larger than any of the settlements we have seen so far," Sybil answered. "There won't be much fun if it isn't."

She pointed toward a cluster of tiny cabins huddled in the shelter of the forest wall. Canoes were drawn up on the beach. "I haven't seen a road or a horse or carriage. Only canoes! How do folks get about from place to place?"

"By canoe, of course!" Roger Conant said, joining the girls. "Swift and silent and muscle developing!"

Halfway down the Sound the sloops put in at a pretty little harbor and Seattle lay before them. Mercer stood gazing at the settlement with such pride and affection that his gaunt, sober features were transformed.

"Seattle!" he cried, flinging out an arm toward the town. "Queen City of the Pacific. Like Rome, built upon seven hills. Like Athens, crowned with marble halls of learning!"

Worth Barton grinned at Abbie. "He means the university yonder. I haven't seen the Parthenon, but I seriously doubt—"

"Oh, Worth!" Abbie reproved him. "It's a lovely building! San Francisco had nothing like it. I don't blame him for being proud."

"I just hope those hills hide some rich veins of coal!" the young man muttered. "Then I'll agree that this is a region to crow about."

The *Maria* was the first of the sloops to reach the small wooden jetty. As her hawsers were flung to waiting hands, a cheer rent the air, and a brass band blared forth with loud, martial music. The people on the dock shouted and waved. From all directions others came running to join them.

Abbie turned to Worth. "What a wonderful welcome!"

she cried. "Oh, they are glad to see us. Isn't it thrilling?"

"There's Hortense! Oh, Mamma! See!" Sybil grabbed her mother's arm. Leaning over the rail she screamed, "Hortense! Halloo! Hortense!" She turned from the rail. "Hurry, Mamma!" she said and then joined the passengers who were pushing eagerly toward the head of the gangway.

Abbie glanced up at Worth. "I mustn't lose her," she said, half apologetically.

"And I'm not going to lose you," Worth answered. "This town isn't big enough to hide you from me for long. All of Washington Territory couldn't do that. So run along with Sybil. I'll find you later."

Happiness flooded Abbie. She had been half afraid, though she had not admitted it even to herself, that once they reached their destination, Worth would be off about his prospecting and she would be forgotten. Now Seattle held a richer promise than she had hoped.

She ran lightly down the gangplank to where Hortense was waiting, arms upstretched, to embrace her mother and sister.

Abbie stood back a little, watching. How wonderful it must be to have a family! To have someone who loved you so much! But she had scarcely time for the thought when Hortense turned to her.

"Abbie Cabot! Welcome, dear. I was so happy when Mamma wrote that you'd be coming with her. You'll love it here, I know. And here's John!" She turned to a tall, tanned man in a plaid woolen shirt. "Mamma, Sybil, Abbie, this is my husband, John Carter."

There was no doubt about the genial welcome in the man's eyes as he greeted his new relatives. In a moment he turned to Abbie.

"You'll come out to the cabin with us, of course! They've made arrangements for all Mercer's party to be cared for at the hotel or in private homes. And of course we spoke for you!"

Abbie felt tears of emotion sting her eyelids at the warmth of the invitation. "If I won't be a bother—" she murmured.

"I've a canoe over here," John said. "We'll all pile into it and go home. The boys can come back for your luggage after it's unloaded."

"The boys?" Sybil asked curiously.

"Our Indians," Hortense explained. "Some of them are much more than boys, but it's easier to call them all that."

Mrs. Wright spoke worriedly. "Is it safe, Hortense, to have Indians work for you? Can they be trusted?"

"Oh, yes, Mamma!" Hortense assured her. "We haven't had any Indian troubles since I've been here, nor for nearly ten years before that! Even then, when there was trouble, Chief Seattle's people were friendly."

Abbie thought back to the various tribes of Plains Indians that had threatened the army outposts where she had lived as a child with her parents.

"It's so peaceful here," she said. "I suppose the Indians wouldn't be as wild and warlike as the Sioux or the Utes."

"There's always a warlike faction, I suppose," John said. "Those who won't sit by quietly while the white men take their lands. But the Dwamish and Suquamish tribes of Chief Seattle have generally been friendly and have observed the treaties our government has signed with them."

They were making their way through the people who had gathered to welcome "Mercer's Belles," or to observe the landing of the passengers from the sloops. Suddenly Carter stopped and called, "Dr. Maynard! You must meet our new citizens!"

As the introductions were made, Abbie carefully observed the man's twinkly blue eyes, with laughter wrinkles at the corners. And a doctor! If she ever got an opportunity to appeal to him, he might help her find work.

They went along the beach, where many canoes were drawn up. Abbie stared at the vessels. They had looked queer from the deck of the *Maria,* nothing like the birch-bark canoes she had been taught to associate with eastern tribes. These canoes were of wood. Many looked like huge single logs with the center burned or hacked out. Many had no thwarts, and Abbie supposed the oarsmen must kneel or squat in this hollow portion as they manipulated the oars. Both ends of the canoes were shaped high and squarish, and the whole painted in bright colors.

They came to John's canoe and he helped them into the craft, which proved roomy enough and was comfortably provided with thwarts. Two muscular Indian youths pushed the little vessel into the water and then leaped in. They grasped the long oars and began to row.

Mrs. Wright and her daughters were eagerly exchanging news and gossip, so Abbie looked about her, taking in the busy scene along the waterfront. The other two

door was open the Indians walked right in and sat down, so someone had the clever idea of making this kind of door. We can open the top for air and sunshine, and leave the bottom tightly shut. The Indians are properly baffled."

The large room was pleasant with its earthen floor covered with bright Indian mats. The furniture—chairs and table and wide bed—were all made of rough lumber. At one end of the room was a huge stone fireplace, and near it stood a small iron stove with a railing around the top. Hortense went to the stove.

"This is John's wedding present to me—a ship's stove, bought from a vessel that stopped here. It's the joy of my life and the envy of my neighbors."

She insisted that her guests relax while she prepared the midday dinner. Halfway through the meal, Mrs. Wright laid down her fork.

"It's charming out here, Hortense," she said slowly, "but isn't it dangerous to be so far from town? Not because of Indians, exactly. But in case of sickness?" She gave her daughter a meaningful look.

Hortense blushed. "If and when I need a doctor, Mamma, Doc Maynard will come, fast. So don't worry."

Abbie and Sybil exchanged glances. A baby—no wonder Hortense had begged her mother to come West!

John said, "You know the government lets a man take up one hundred and sixty acres of land—and his wife the same amount. This was the finest, richest soil I could find. And while it is out a little way now, someday, I'm positive, it will be very close, maybe right in the town."

"But does the government have a right to let you take

this land?" Abbie asked curiously. "Doesn't it belong to the Indians?"

"Yes, and the government has recognized that fact and has acquired title through various treaties and payments. Oh, I'll admit that there are many faults in the treaties—we get the best of it, of course. But it was necessary for us to occupy this land or the British surely would have done so."

After dinner, Mrs. Wright went to the room John had built onto the cabin for her and Sybil. "It's large enough for you, too, Abbie" Hortense insisted.

Abbie could see that it would be very crowded, and she made up her mind then and there not to impose too long on the generosity of these friends.

When the canoes returned with the trunks, Abbie and Sybil set to work pressing ruffles and ribbons so they would look their best for the party.

It was still light when they entered Yesler's Hall that evening, but already pine-knot torches were flaring from sconces, candles were alight on long tables, and women were bustling about placing dishes and food. Hortense excused herself and joined the busy hostesses. Sybil scanned the little clusters of men standing around the hall, obviously dressed in their best.

"I wonder where Rod is?" she said, using the nickname the popular reporter had insisted upon during the voyage.

"Maybe he and Worth aren't invited," Mrs. Wright said. "I understand this is really a party for the bachelors of the Territory!" She regarded the two girls, her eyes merry with mischief. "I don't think those bachelors would particularly welcome two young men who have had three months' handicap!"

Just then one of Mercer's girls, Ida May Barlow, came into the hall on the arm of a stranger.

"Look!" Abbie whispered. "Who can that be with Ida May? She didn't know a soul out here—"

"But Asa Mercer knows everyone. And Ida May and Annie Stephens are chums," Sybil said. "I'll wager my black velvet neck ribbon that Mr. Mercer brings Annie, and that he has arranged for Ida May to have an escort!"

"And there's Mrs. Peterson with a partner!" Mrs. Wright observed. "I wonder if he knows what little demons her children are."

John Carter looked at them quizzically. "You'll have partners, never fear. Asa has planned this shindig to the last detail. It is his hour of triumph—even though he brought only one tenth of his promised five hundred."

Sure enough, Asa Mercer was making his way toward them with Annie Stephens on his arm, and a trio of husky men behind him.

"The bearded one's for you, Mamma," Sybil said with a giggle. "We'll have to draw lots, Abbie, for the other two."

"If I thought Worth would be coming—" Abbie began, but John Carter shook his head. "You'll have to be nice to the local boys, tonight at least," he admonished.

Mercer stopped in front of them. "Good evening, ladies! John!" He barely nodded to include Carter. "May I introduce some of my Seattle friends, who would like to escort you to dinner and to the ball afterward? I can vouch for their respectability," he added pompously.

The girls smiled faintly, but Mrs. Wright's voice was warm as she said, "That's very kind of you, Mr. Mercer. I'm sure John is eager to join his wife and do what he can to help."

Mercer beamed and reeled off the introductions. The older, bearded man was Dell Cushing; the tall, lanky young fellow was Tolley Heaton; and the shorter, jolly-faced one was Philip Strang. Cushing seemed more assured than the other two. He spoke quietly to Mrs. Wright, and with a smiling farewell to the girls, she placed her hand on his arm and moved away.

The two young men stood tongue-tied and flushed. The girls hesitated, the same thought in both minds: Would Worth and Rod come? Asa Mercer's bright blue eyes looked piercingly into Abbie's.

"Miss Cabot," he said meaningfully, "Mr. Heaton is waiting. I suggest—"

Abbie stiffened. Why should Asa Mercer think he could suggest what partner she should have? Suddenly she knew why. He wanted her to hurry up and find a husband who would pay off her note! A curt refusal sprang to her lips, but John Carter laid his hand gently on her shoulder.

"The men have been looking forward to this party for a long time," he said quietly. "It is the highlight of years for them. You can enjoy it, too."

With a slight shrug, Abbie shook off her annoyance. After all, it wasn't this fellow's fault that she owed Mercer so much. She looked up at Tolley and smiled.

"Thank you, Mr. Heaton," she said.

Sybil had accepted the round-faced young man's arm, and they all moved off toward the tables.

Just then Worth and Roger came into the hall. They looked around, found the two girls and started toward them. Asa Mercer stopped them.

"The tables at this end of the hall are reserved for Seattle men with female partners," he said crisply. "The unaccompanied men will sit together at the other end."

"Oh, now, Mercer!" Worth said indignantly, "that's not fair. The party's for your passengers—and as for partners, we'll have them if you give us a chance."

"You're mistaken," Mercer answered. "You are not one of my passengers. And even if you were, this dinner is for but one purpose—to let my Seattle friends get acquainted with the ladies I brought out here."

Abbie and Sybil glanced at each other. They had accepted partners and there was nothing they could do now. They went along to the decorated tables and seated themselves.

When the meal was over, the plank tables were cleared and removed. Young boys scattered corn meal over the wooden floor and scuffed across it, laughing. "Makes the floor slick for dancing," Tolley Heaton explained. He was a nimble dancer, and Abbie was flushed and laughing when Worth came to claim the second dance.

"So!" he began angrily when they were on the floor, "you've wasted no time picking out a lumberjack! I suppose he's one of Mercer's cronies, and well supplied with the wherewithal to pay off your note!"

Abbie stopped in the middle of the floor. "If you are going to be disagreeable, you can take me back to my partner!" she said. Not for worlds would she have told him how she had tried to wait for his coming.

Worth laughed suddenly. When he spoke it was in his old, bantering tone. "You evidently don't know me yet, Miss Cabot! I'm not giving you back to him at all! at all!"

Abbie's lashes hid the candid gray eyes. She didn't want him to see how pleased she was. If only he could dance with her all night, as they had so often danced on the ship. But he couldn't. Asa Mercer would see to that. She relaxed in the gaiety of the quadrille, in the joy of having Worth's strong arms swing her about till she was laughing and giddy with delight.

As soon as that set was finished, Dr. Maynard came bustling up to claim her for the next dance. "I can't wait to enjoy a set with the prettiest girl Asa Mercer found back East," he said, his eyes twinkling.

When she conveniently could, Abbie broached the subject that had lain, only half-buried in her thoughts, all day.

"Dr. Maynard," she began, "my friend Hortense Carter tells me you have a hospital here—"

"A small one. A very small one—just a part of my house," the doctor said.

"Don't you need help? I desperately need a job—"

"I do, I do, indeed! Mrs. Maynard and old Chief Seattle's daughter Angeline are all the help I have. And Angeline can't be counted on much. Yes, we need help, what with all the accidents to the lumberjacks, burns from those detestable fish oil lamps that are constantly setting something or someone on fire. Injuries from encounters with wild animals or hostile Indians—we do have some that take a delight in mischief. To say nothing of the ague and fevers, sore throats and infections. Need help? My dear child, everyone here needs help. That's why Asa went East—to bring back women to supply this need."

"Then I'm not afraid to ask—will you give me a job?"

"Are you, by any lucky chance, a nurse. Miss Cabot?"

"I wish I were. But I have worked in a hospital—a famous one. The Boston General—"

"Wonderful!" the doctor began, but Abbie cut him short.

"I just did what my old friend called slopwork," she explained. "I scrubbed floors, washed bedding and—emptied slops—"

Dr. Maynard drew back a little to look at her. "My dear! That's what Angeline does—"

"And she's a chief's daughter—a princess!" Abbie pointed out triumphantly. "I'm nothing so fine."

Dr. Maynard's laugh rang out, so loud that people turned to look at them.

"Angeline's a princess, I suppose, but Queen Victoria wouldn't recognize her!"

"I don't want to take her place," Abbie said earnestly, "but there are many things I could do. If you'll just try me, sir. I do need work. I have signed a note to pay Mr. Mercer three hundred dollars for my passage here, and I want to discharge that debt as rapidly as possible."

"Well, child, I will do what I can to help you. However, I must warn you that we don't make much money in my hospital. Many of the Indians can't pay anything;

many of the settlers pay in food or labor. But if you want
to come and take what I can pay—"

"A room and my food and just a little money—"

"Come tomorrow and talk to Catherine, my wife. We'll
see what we can do."

"Thank you, sir!" Abbie said gratefully. "I can't ask
for anything more."

When Dr. Maynard returned her to her little group
she threw her arms about Sybil.

"Oh, Sybil!" she whispered excitedly. "I've found a
job—I'm sure I've got a job, already! Asa Mercer doesn't
need to hunt up a husband for me!"

# 6 ◄◄◄◄◄◄◄◄◄◄◄◄◄◄◄◄◄◄◄◄◄◄◄◄◄◄◄◄◄◄

THE NEXT MORNING, ABBIE MADE HER WAY up the sloping main street of Seattle, toward the bluff on which stood the long, low house she hoped would be her next home. When she had explained her purpose and her hopes, her friends had expressed regret at losing her. But they understood the necessity and wished her success. John was making a trip into the settlement and she had come to town with him.

"That's Doc's house on that bluff south of town," John said, pointing. "He has a wonderful view of the Sound. But, Abbie," he regarded her seriously, "if you don't like it, or if it proves too much for you, come back to us. We'll always have room for you, and be glad to have you."

As Abbie reached the brow of the hill she saw the fenced-in garden in front of the house. She paused to look at it—to identify the vegetables and flowers that luxuriated in the rich soil. She smiled at the plot of dandelions—no one in Boston would tolerate such a thing. But Hortense had told her that Catherine Maynard cultivated dandelions as a remedy for many of the commoner ailments.

She went through the gate and up onto a wide porch.

74

Before knocking she turned to glimpse the view John had mentioned. Below her stretched the blue waters of the Sound, dotted with tiny green islets and rimmed by forest-covered slopes. Far beyond, in the distant east rose snowy Mount Rainier and to the west lay the glistening peaks of the coastal range. It was a breath-takingly lovely scene.

The door was opened by a frail-looking woman, not much taller than Abbie. She gave the girl one quick glance and held out her hand, smiling.

"You must be Abbie Cabot! The doctor told me you'd be coming. I was sorry to miss you yesterday, but I've not been too well, so I didn't go down to the dock, nor to the party last night. But come in, come in, my dear! Dr. Maynard is busy right now, but he will be with us as soon as possible."

Abbie liked the woman. She was intelligent and friendly. It would be pleasant to work with her.

They chatted easily. Catherine Maynard asked about the voyage and about Abbie's life in Boston. Then Dr. Maynard joined them, jovial as ever, though his eyes were blurred with weariness. Abbie had seen the same look on her father's face after he had been through a particularly difficult night.

"How are you, my dear?" the doctor asked. "Haven't changed your mind, then? Catherine, have you explained what she'll be doing? Has she met Angeline?"

"I waited for you to tell her, David. She really doesn't look as if she's used to heavy work—"

"Oh, but I am!" Abbie hastened to interrupt. "It's just that three months on the ship have taken away the traces. And it doesn't matter one bit what you want me to do, I'll do it!"

"Well," Mrs. Maynard said, "it will be mostly keeping the rooms and bedding clean, seeing that there's always hot water, maybe helping some with handling the patients. You'll have Angeline to help you. But one word of caution, Abbie. The Chief's daughter is known as a hellcat! I'm about the only person who can handle her when her temper's roused. So you'll have to be careful not to stir her up."

"Bring her in, Catherine," the doctor suggested. "Let Abbie get acquainted with the cross she's going to have to bear. Doubtless, Angeline will be more difficult even than the work you do."

Catherine Maynard went to the door and called "Princess Angeline! Come here, please!"

Abbie was thrilled at the thought of meeting a real Indian princess. She looked toward the door, eager to see the woman, and she was not prepared at all for the short, shapeless figure that entered. Angeline's face was the color of old, worn leather, crumpled into deep wrinkles. The toothless mouth hung loose, an old bandanna wrapped the head. Oh, Abbie thought, she must have on a dozen skirts!

None of Abbie's surprise showed as she made a slight, formal curtsy and smiled at the old woman. Angeline was pleased at this obvious respect.

"*Kloshe skaik hlentkhl*," she muttered.

The doctor beamed. "You've passed muster. She says you are a good girl."

In Chinook Catherine Maynard explained to the old Indian that Abbie was to live with them and help with the work. Then she said, "Now come, child, let me show you your room. It will have to be just the attic—there's no place else. But it will be yours alone."

Abbie smiled. "I haven't had a room to myself for more than three years. Anything will be fine."

She followed Mrs. Maynard up a ladder and into the small, shadowy room. There was no window, but the logs hadn't been too well chinked, and a good deal of light filtered in through the cracks. Only in the center could Abbie stand upright, but she didn't mind.

"You'll want to go back to Hortense's and let your friends know that it's all settled," Catherine Maynard said. "You can bring your clothes and things tomorrow and by that time we'll have a cot up here and a basin. It isn't much—"

"It's a room of my own and a job!" Abbie said with enthusiasm. "I'll be happy here, I know."

They came down the ladder to be met by howls and curses coming from behind a closed door. Catherine ran forward and flung the door open. Abbie, at her heels, saw Angeline angrily pulling bedding from a narrow cot. A gaunt, bearded man lay on the floor, shouting at the princess. When he saw Catherine he bawled, "She's a devil, that's what she is! Where's the doc? She's killed me! She's killed me for sure!"

"Now, now, Jake!" Catherine soothed, bending over the man. Her hands ran rapidly over his meager frame. "You're not hurt. I'll get you back into bed. Abbie, child, you'll find some clean blankets in a chest in the hall. Will you get a couple and spread them on the cot. Then help me lift Jake, here, onto it?"

Abbie hurried to do as asked, but she wondered. Not a word of reproof had been said to Angeline, who had gone muttering from the room, her arms filled with the bedding. It took only a moment to find the chest, extract the blankets and spread them on the cot. Lifting Jake was not difficult, either, because he was so thin. All the time he kept yelling invectives against Angeline and calling for the doctor.

Catherine answered patiently. "The doctor has been called away, Jake. I'll tell him about this when he comes back. Now just lie back and relax. There! There! I'll get you a plug of tobacco. How'll that be?"

Jake subsided, still grumbling a little, but when the tobacco was in his hand, he stopped talking in order to chew.

"What did Angeline do that for?" Abbie asked.

"Oh," Catherine said, "there's a lasting feud between them. Jake has been here for some time, he's now convalescing from scurvy. We got him off a whaling vessel which had been a long time up North. Several of the men were suffering somewhat, but Jake was so bad they left him here. For some reason he took a dislike to having Angeline around him, and she responds by handling him roughly." She shrugged. "He'll be discharged as soon as possible."

"I should think he'd want to be!" Abbie declared, her shock giving way to amusement.

"We have only one other patient right now," Catherine

Maynard said. "An Indian woman who was attacked after the party last night. Some rowdies from the North, Haidas, I suppose, came down here. They tried to grab the basket of food she was taking home from the party. She resisted and they cut her up some. She's in here."

Catherine opened a door and Abbie looked in on a heavy-set squaw, swathed in bandages, lying on a low cot. Her breath came in hoarse, rasping gasps, but she was sleeping. Catherine closed the door.

"I suppose you wonder why I did not reprimand Angeline," she said. "Well, we have been friends for years. The doctor and I lived on the Dwamish reservation at one time. There was an uprising, and Angeline and her father saved my life. Since then we have been blood sisters. I am very fond of her, in spite of her wild ways. She was a spoiled child, and she learned to swear from 'King George's men' as the Indians call British sailors. But underneath she is a true friend to the white settlers, and I'm fond of her," she repeated.

Abbie soon learned that the Maynards had not exaggerated the difficulties of her work in the hospital. She rose at the first streak of dawn, dressed swiftly and descended to the kitchen to prepare breakfast, while Mrs. Maynard bathed the patients and prepared them for their meal. Both had ravenous appetites and were surly when they could not have all they wanted to eat.

Jake tried wheedling when Abbie started to take away the empty tray. "Yer a pretty li'l thing, miss! Ye look to have a good heart. Ye wouldn't let a man starve, now, would ye?"

The Dwamish squaw grunted ferociously. Abbie was glad to escape to the kitchen. When the patients were quieted, the Maynards had their own breakfast, Abbie eating with them. Angeline, in spite of her royal blood, ate alone, squatting on the back doorstep.

Then the rooms had to be cleaned and aired, the washing done in a huge iron kettle over a fire in the yard. If the sun was shining, she spread the sheets and blankets on the grass to dry. If, as so often happened, it was raining, the wet things were draped over chairs and hung from lines in the kitchen. Then Abbie had to carry wood to keep the fire blazing so that the needed bedding would dry.

After the midday meal, she helped Catherine or the doctor change the dressings on the squaw's slashed arms and back. She gave old Jake his required lemon juice. If there was time, she cooked and bottled the wild berries brought to the door by Indians. At night she wearily climbed the ladder and fell onto her cot, exhausted. But she slept soundly and awoke ready for another day.

Abbie was out in the yard boiling bandages. Material, especially linen, was difficult to obtain, and used bandages had to be boiled and bleached for reuse. To protect her calico skirt from the grass, wet by last night's rain, she had folded it up from the bottom and pinned it at the back. Her petticoat showed. Her cheeks were smudged with soot and her hair, loosened by her activity, lay in perspiration-damp curls on her forehead. Her lungs were full of the smothery smell of hot lye soap and burning cedar wood.

"I'm a sight!" she muttered. "I'm glad we're up here

on the bluff. Down in town, passers-by would get an eye-
ful of this Mercer Belle!" She leaned over the kettle on
the fire and stirred the bandages with a long stick.

Just then she was seized from behind and whirled off
her feet. A hearty kiss was planted upon her damp neck.
She didn't have to see who it was, but happiness at
Worth's visit lost the battle with chagrin at being caught
in such disarray.

"Put me down!" she cried. "Put me down!"

Worth held her close for a moment, then set her on
her feet. She reached behind her to unpin her skirt,
fumbling in her annoyance.

"This is a horrible time to come calling!" she scolded.
"Just look at me—no, don't! Oh, what a nuisance!"

Worth laughed happily. "You are a pretty sight, my
dear. A pretty sight for any man. It's good you know
how to wash clothes! As Tolley Heaton's wife, I'll wager
you'll have plenty of that to do!" His tone was teasing, his
eyes affectionate and tender.

"You might have let me know you were coming!"

"How could I?" he asked reasonably. "I didn't know
where you were. Rod and I rented a canoe and rowed
out to the Carters' cabin. Lord, what muscle straining!
They told me you were here, so I came back to find you.
I left Rod out there, telling Sybil good-by."

Abbie forgot her discomfiture. "Good-by! Is Rod leaving so soon?"

"Yes. The *Maria* returns to San Francisco tomorrow
and Rod will be on it. Ah, I imagine the girls will all
miss him. Unless, like someone I know, they have picked
out a replacement. Come!" He took her hand and led her

to the back porch. They sat down side by side on the lower step.

"Oh, why doesn't he stay?" Abbie asked. "He could get a job on the paper here. From what I've seen of it, the Puget Sound *Daily* could do with a reporter like Rod."

"He's a New Yorker. This frontier life doesn't appeal to him."

"You're staying, though?" Abbie asked.

"I sure am. Going to get rich out here—make my own fortune, so my father can keep his. But—Abbie, I won't be here in Seattle. I've been talking to men around town and studying maps and records, and I think I know where I should start looking for coal. After Rod leaves tomorrow, I'll set out. I've got my gear together and an Indian guide—"

"Where will you go? How long will you be?"

Worth shook his head. "Who knows? First off I'm going up on the Black River. Years ago a Dr. Bigelow discovered coal on his land but he had no capital to develop his claim. Maybe it wasn't worth developing. I don't know. But I'm going up there to find out."

"I wish you luck," Abbie said.

"As soon as I locate my claim, I'll come back and then, Abbie, darling, we'll be married!" His arm went around her and he drew her close. As he bent to kiss her she drew back.

"You forget, Worth! I'm not free to marry. I owe Asa Mercer three hundred dollars—"

"Oh, that!" Worth tossed the idea aside. "You can forget that note. If I find a claim—"

Abbie's back stiffened. "It's my debt. I'll pay it!"

"Well, let's not argue about a trifle—"

"Trifle! Worth, it's three hundred dollars. It will take a long time—maybe two years—for me to pay that back."

"And it may take two years for me to find coal!" Worth declared. He drew her close. "Abbie, darling! I've loved you ever since that day when I first saw you. No," he corrected honestly, "I didn't really love you then. It was when Asa Mercer dragged you out of that sewing room —your hair awry, your eyes wide with alarm. You looked such a little, terrified girl—"

"I wasn't terrified. I was just chagrined and, well, maybe a little scared. Mercer looked so mad I thought he might throw me overboard."

They smiled at the remembrance. "You'll marry me, then?"

"I don't know, Worth! It will be such a long time—" Worth had to be content with that.

The next morning Abbie and Sybil and a number of the *Continental* passengers were on hand to bid Roger Conant farewell. Sybil was miserable, her dark eyes enormous in her pale face.

"I don't know what I'll do when he's gone!" she told Abbie. "I've grown so used to him. He was such fun! Remember the day we went ashore at Rio? The picnic on the beach and all? I love him, Abbie. And I thought he loved me—"

"He's fond of you, darling," Abbie consoled her friend. "But Rod always said he was just going to come here with us and then return to New York. He's told us about his family, and his invalid brother and how his mother counts on him—"

"I know. But I hoped. Oh, Abbie, how I hoped he would stay, anyway!"

Roger, too, was sad. "This has been the greatest experience of my whole life. I'll never forget you all!" he told the girls fluttering around him. He turned to Sybil. "And you, Sybil, my sweet, have been the dearest, the loveliest, the hardest to part from." He took her in his arms and kissed her gently. "I don't know how I'll ever bear it!"

"But he did bear it!" Sybil moaned, as the *Maria* sailed out of sight. "He did bear it! I'm the one that can't—"

"Don't cry, Sybil!" Abbie begged. She ached with sympathy. But tomorrow, she, too, would be alone. Yet it was different. Worth loved her and he was staying. If only she didn't owe Mercer she'd be the happiest girl alive. But if she didn't owe Mercer, she wouldn't be here—and she would never have known Worth.

"Things work out, Sybil!" she comforted. "Usually, things work out all right."

# 7 ‹‹‹‹‹‹‹‹‹‹‹‹‹‹‹‹‹‹‹‹‹‹‹‹‹‹‹‹‹‹‹‹‹‹‹‹‹‹‹‹

As the June days lengthened, a heat spell descended on the region. Everyone complained. "Hottest month we've ever had!" they declared, mopping steaming brows. Those who were well just grumbled and sought the shade. The patients in the hospital tossed and groaned. Abbie had her hands full, soothing the perspiration-soaked bodies, fighting hordes of flies, trying to comfort the miserable.

At night, shut up in her tiny attic room, she felt as though she were in a perpetual steam bath. She could not sleep. Under the pressure of work and heat the bloom left her cheeks and she began to look as pale and weary as Catherine Maynard.

One night, finding the attic unbearable, she took her pillow and sheet and went down to the front porch. She would just sleep there in the outdoors, where there was at least a whisper of air.

Before lying down she stood for a moment by the porch rail, looking out over the Sound. It was a beautiful night, calm and still, with an eerie luminescence that seemed to radiate from sky and sea and beach. And there was something else. A sound—a scarcely discernible sound.

Abbie listened intently. It was the sound of drums. Somewhere, in the distance, drums were beating in a slow, sad rhythm. As she recognized this, she heard also the low, almost inaudible music of human tones, muted by distance to an indistinct hum. It was mournful and weird. What could it be?

She was still standing there, wondering, when she saw the familiar figure of Dr. Maynard toiling up the path to the house. He came through the gate and up onto the porch. Then he saw Abbie and came toward her.

"What is it?" she asked, "that sound of drums and a sort of chant?"

"The Indians," Maynard answered. "Old Chief Seattle has just died. I was over there with him. The Indians are mourning for their chieftain."

"Angeline!" Abbie cried softly. "What about Angeline?"

"She is with her father's body. I took her with me when I went. Oh, but she will miss him. She was always his closest companion. He had wanted a son to be chieftain after him, but he never let on to his daughter. He treated her as much like a son as possible."

"Had he no other children?"

"None but Angeline by his first wife. He has four or five by his second wife, but they don't count. I've never been able to figure it out, but this second family isn't considered in the hierarchy."

He glanced at the pillow and sheet. "Too hot in the attic, eh? Well, tomorrow we can move your cot out here if you like. And tomorrow will be the Chief's funeral. Oh, yes! Tolley Heaton asked me to tell you that he'd be over to take you to the ceremonies."

"Tolley Heaton? How—"

"He works for Meigs, at the mill. And Meigs was old Seattle's closest neighbor and friend. Naturally Tolley was there when the old man died. He thought you'd like to see an Indian burial ceremony. Everyone will be there—"

Abbie hesitated. "Couldn't I go with you and Catherine?"

"Of course you can, if that's what you want. But it will be pretty disappointing to Tolley to row clear over here to get you, only to find that you won't go with him. He's a good boy, Abbie, has the makings of a fine man. He'll be with young folks—I really think you'd enjoy the day more with him than with us old fogies."

Abbie made up her mind. "Of course I'll go with Tolley. It was kind of him to think of me."

"Well, do as you like, Abbie, child. I'm turning in. It's been quite a night. Nothing I could do for the old man, and I knew it was coming. But you always hate to see a friend go, and Seattle was a friend, always, to us." He turned and shuffled wearily into the house.

When Tolley came for her the next day, Abbie was ready. She was wearing her lavender-sprigged dimity, freshly laundered. She looked crisp and cool. Fortunately there were no patients in the hospital today, and the Maynards had left early. Catherine's affection for the bereaved princess had drawn her to the Old Man House to do what she could for the family.

Tolley beamed down on Abbie. "You look mighty nice, ma'am. That's a mighty pretty dress you're wearing."

"Thank you, Tolley!" she said, dimpling. "You look mighty nice yourself."

It was a fact, she thought. He did look much handsomer in his plaid woolen shirt, the open collar showing the tanned column of his neck, the sleeves rolled up over brown, muscular arms. His manner was easier, too, than it had been at the party, and she realized suddenly that it must have been the unaccustomed dress-up clothing that had embarrassed him.

It was a fifteen-mile canoe trip across the Sound and through Agate Pass to the far shore where Old Man House stood. As they passed Port Madison, Tolley proudly pointed out the lumber mill.

"That's where I work and live. Meigs's mill. We turn out some mighty good lumber. A lot of the houses around here are made from our stuff."

"It looks as if everyone's coming to the funeral!" Abbie motioned toward the canoes which seemed to fill the blue waters of the Sound, their painted sides gleaming in the sunlight. Overhead flocks of white-winged gulls soared; their raucous cries cut across the splash of oars, the murmur of conversation, and the ripples of laughter.

"I'll bet there'll be five hundred people here today," Tolley said. "I thought you'd like seeing them and the ceremony. He was a great man, Seattle, and they're doing right to show him honor."

"There's Mr. Mercer with Annie Stephens," Abbie cried, as they passed the small canoe holding the couple.

"Yes, ma'am," Tolley said with a grin. "Folks say as how there'll be a wedding soon."

"And Ida May Barlow with the man that brought her to the party. Bert Pinkham, Catherine said his name is. I wonder how they managed to get so well acquainted so fast."

"Nothing funny about it," her companion said. "All of us unmarried men were at the dock when the sloops came in. I guess he just picked her out, same as I picked you."

Abbie smiled. "I'm flattered, Tolley."

"And then Bert's a kind of impatient fellow. He doesn't want to wait—to give the girl a chance to look around a bit. I guess he feels he has a right to get right down to brass tacks with no fooling around."

Abbie's eyes flew from the bright scene to her companion's face. "A right? What do you mean?"

"Well, us fellows that gave Asa three hundred dollars to bring us back a wife, we had first choice. And I guess Bert just thought he'd—"

Abbie's eyes widened with shock and disbelief. "Three hundred dollars? Tolley, did you give Asa Mercer three hundred dollars to—to—" She could not say it.

Tolley stared at her, his face reddening.

"You were buying a wife!" she cried.

"Now don't get mad, Miss Abbie. It wasn't like that at all. Asa said maybe some nice girls wouldn't have the money to pay their fare, and if we wanted to be sure that we'd have someone, it would be an act of charity to pay their way. I wanted a wife," he went on soberly. "I don't deny it. So I chipped in my money. And as soon as I saw you on the deck there I said to myself, that's the one. So—"

"So you think you have paid for me!" Abbie choked on the words. "Oh, if I'd known that I'd never, never have let you even speak to me!" She bit her lip, trying to hold back the angry tears.

She knew that one of the purposes of Mercer's expedition was to provide possible wives for the unmarried men in the Territory. *Possible* wives! She hadn't dreamed that some of the men had actually purchased the right to claim any of the passengers. At a sudden thought her shock gave way to anger.

"If you paid for my passage, then I don't owe Asa Mercer anything! That note I signed! It's you I owe, and it's you I'll pay! Oh, that man! People said not to trust him!"

"Now, now, Miss Abbie. Don't take on so!" Tolley said. He was both angry and contrite—angry that Abbie was accusing him of a sort of skulduggery, contrite that he had hurt her feelings. "You don't owe me a cent and you're not obligated to accept my offer. I'd have been glad to help you out, whether you like me or not. But don't hold it against Asa, either. He's honest. He told me about your note and said he'd tear it up if we got married. I'm sorry we had to talk about this today. I wanted to give you time to get to know me. Now you'll not be likely to trust any of us. But we were all just doing what we could. We didn't mean any harm or insult."

The handsome face before her was puckered like a child's, a child who was trying to look brave though he had been mortally hurt. Abbie couldn't stand that look. She reached out her hand and touched Tolley's arm.

"I'm sorry, too. I don't want to spoil the day. Let's forget it for now."

But Abbie couldn't forget it. When she saw Sybil with Phil Strang she couldn't help asking, "Did Philip Strang pay Mercer, too?"

"Yes," he answered.

"But Sybil's mother paid their way!"

"Listen, Miss Abbie. Don't fret about it. Asa Mercer doesn't intend to rob anyone. If a fellow's given him money but gets a wife that's paid her own way, Asa will fix it right. It may take a little time. He's lost everything and is in debt right up to his ears. But he'll pay. I know him. You've known him for some time, too. Can't you tell that he's honest?"

"Yes," Abbie admitted slowly. "Only this has rather shaken me up."

Tolley beached the canoe and helped Abbie out. In silence they made their way toward Sybil and Phil.

"Did your mother come?" Abbie asked.

"Yes, Mr. Cushing brought her. And Hortense and John are here somewhere. My, you look sober, Abbie. What's the matter?"

"Nothing," Abbie fibbed.

The crowd was moving up the slope toward a huge log structure.

"Just what is Old Man House?" Sybil asked. "Do they call it that because the Chief lived there?"

Phil chuckled. "Not exactly. It's a sort of common house for the whole tribe. It was built seventy years ago, when the Chief was a boy, and it has forty apartments in it. The Indians say that after the white man came— Vancouver, it was, in his ship *Discovery*—the Dwamish felt their huts were a disgrace. So they decided to build a great potlatch house—something the white man would have to admire and wonder at. The greatest house in the world, they said. That's it, in front of us."

The body of the old Chief lay, blanket-covered, on a leafy bier in front of his home.

"There's an altar and a priest!" Abbie said. "I didn't know these Indians were Christians."

"Oh, yes," Phil said. "Seattle was baptized a Catholic long ago." Tolley remained silent and Abbie realized he was as hurt as she was shocked.

The priest began to perform the rites to which the old Chief was entitled, and the crowd became silent. As the Mass ended and the priest genuflected and turned from the altar, a subchief stepped forward.

He raised one hand high, his bronzed body gleaming against the weathered logs of the Old Man House.

*"See-at-lee! See-at-lee! See-at-lee!"* he cried in a rich, guttural voice.

"That's what the Indians called Seattle!" Phil whispered.

"A-a'h! A-a'h! A-a'h!" came in a moan from the tribesmen.

Angeline was sitting near the bier, rocking her body back and forth. *"Hyas Papa! Hyas Papa!"* she shrieked.

"A-a'h! A-a'h! A-a'h! moaned the others.

The subchief waited a moment. Then he began to speak. In a solemn voice he recounted the main events in the life of Seattle and the great Chief's accomplishments.

As he enumerated each deed, Angeline shrieked, *"Hyas Papa!"*

Finally the subchief paused. "But why do I speak? The great Chief's son is here. Let us hear his voice!"

A tall Indian who had been sitting near Angeline rose and stepped forward. Abbie turned to Tolley.

"Dr. Maynard said only Angeline was considered of royal blood—" she whispered.

Tolley nodded. "But a woman can't speak at a funeral. So they are recognizing Jim, Angeline's half brother."

Jim also spoke in surprisingly good English as he contrasted the ways of the Dwamish now with those of the days before the white man came. Then he drew from his blanket, folded across his breast, a photograph. He held it out for all to see.

"The white man cannot forget him!" he shouted triumphantly. "See! Here is his picture, made by the light of the heavens. When the Seattles are no longer here, their chief will be remembered. His likeness will be known!"

Forgetting his withdrawal, Tolley whispered, "That's the only picture ever taken of the old Chief. Sammis got it the last time Seattle was in town. It's lucky he did, for I'm sure the Chief's name will go down in history and folks will want to know what he really looked like."

Abbie nodded. She smiled brightly up into the strong face to show Tolley that she was holding no grudge against him.

Six braves stepped forward, lifted the leafy bier and carried it toward the grassy slope above the beach. The old Chief was to be buried there on the ground he loved, in sight of the blue waters he had known so well.

The crowd was breaking up. Abbie and Sybil looked around for Mrs. Wright and Hortense, and the two groups were soon joined.

"Abbie, my dear child!" Mrs. Wright cried. "How are you, dear? We have missed you these past weeks. You look thinner. Are you working too hard?"

Abbie laughed. "I'm fine. The Maynards are wonderful. I've been wanting to come out to your place, Hortense, but we've been busy."

"Can't you come out today? John killed a wild pig yesterday and we'll have a nice roast for dinner. We'll have to pickle most of it, of course, but we're bound to enjoy what we can right now."

"Oh, do come, Abbie!" Sybil urged.

Abbie smiled ruefully. "I'm a working girl, remember?"

Just then Dr. Maynard joined the group.

"Abbie, child, I've been looking for you. Why don't you take the rest of the day off? There's nothing to be done at the hospital. Fortunately we're just out of patients! And Catherine and I are going to stay here with Angeline awhile."

Sybil clapped her hands. "What luck! You're a darling, Doctor. We've just been begging Abbie to come out to the cottage. Now, of course you'll come, Abbie?"

"You boys, too!" John Carter put in. "And Dell, of course. We'll have a real party. And it's so much cooler out there in the forest."

Still Abbie hesitated. She had meant to face Asa Mercer today, while her wrath was hot. But maybe it would be better to wait. Her father had always advised her to cool off a bit before expressing her anger. She turned to Tolley.

"Will you come?"

The tanned face flushed with pleasure. "I'd be plumb delighted, Miss Abbie!"

With a tiny shrug Abbie shook off the last vestige of her annoyance. She took Tolley's arm and, laughing, said, "It sounds wonderful!"

"What are we waiting for then?" John said. "Come along, one and all!"

Laughing and chattering, they made their way down the beach toward the canoes.

# 8 ‹‹‹‹‹‹‹‹‹‹‹‹‹‹‹‹‹‹‹‹‹‹‹‹‹‹‹‹‹‹‹‹‹‹‹‹‹‹

"OH, ANGELINE! I'M GLAD YOU'VE COME!" Abbie welcomed the Chief's daughter a few days after the funeral.

The old woman lumbered into the kitchen and carefully laid down the soiled bundle she always carried.

"Where *doctin?*"

"The doctor and Mrs. Maynard have gone down to Mrs. Blackwell's. Her baby's come." Abbie did not try to talk the jargon of the Indians. She had discovered that many of them, like Angeline, understood quite well what was said, though they might feel it expedient to pretend not to.

Angeline stuck out her lips toward the other rooms of the house. It was her way of pointing.

"Who sick?"

"Only one. Mrs. Ebey. She's not very sick, though. She came in last night with some boils on her shoulders. The *doctin* fixed her up and let her stay a day or two so he could change the dressings. Oh, Angeline, I'm so glad you're here. It's scary to be alone—"

A horrible scream cut the air. Abbie looked at Angeline and then ran.

96

Mrs. Ebey lay in the middle of the floor of her room. Her body was rigid, her face swollen and purple. Saliva tinged with blood foamed on her lips. Abbie stared, shocked and frightened.

"Angeline!"

The old woman was right behind her, standing pushed back against the door, her face livid with terror. She was jabbering in the Chinook jargon that both the Maynards understood so well, but Abbie could not make head or tails of it.

"We must do something!" Abbie cried. "She's chewing her tongue! It's bleeding!"

She forced down her panic and looked around. There was nothing in the room that she could use to put in the woman's mouth to keep her teeth from macerating her tongue. Abbie lifted a corner of her apron and tore off a strip. With trembling fingers she rolled this into a small cylinder. She knelt beside the jerking woman and forced the roll of cloth between her gnashing teeth. Angeline moaned with fear.

Abbie had no idea what else to do. She stood watching the convulsive movements, frightened and ignorant of what had caused the seizure. As she watched, the movements seemed to become less violent, the awful rasping breathing grew a little quieter, the face became less livid. It could not have been five minutes since that scream before Mrs. Ebey lay pale and exhausted and quiet.

Abbie removed the roll of cloth from the woman's relaxed mouth and tossed it aside.

"Help me put her to bed!" she commanded Angeline. The Indian woman approached fearfully, but when she saw that the patient was indeed quiescent, she gingerly helped Abbie lift her and place her on the cot. Abbie covered her with a blanket, felt her pulse and laid her ear over the thudding heart.

"I don't know what else to do!" she said worriedly. "Oh, if only Dr. Maynard would come!"

There was a pounding on the front door and Angeline padded out to see who was there. With one last glance at the resting patient, Abbie followed.

Dan Phillips, owner of the general store, stood there with his young son Tommy. The child was howling.

"Where's the doc?" the father asked anxiously. "We need the doc! In a hurry, Miss Abbie!"

"The doctor's not here. What's wrong?" She thought it couldn't be very bad, the boy was making such a noise.

"Show her, Tommy!"

The youngster held out his right arm. Blood was pumping from the forefinger in deep red spurts. Abbie saw with horror that the tip of the finger was hanging by a slender thread of skin.

"Oh, Tommy! Don't!" Abbie grasped his arm and bent it at the elbow, so that the wounded hand was upright. "Angeline! bring some cold water. Why did you let him carry his hand down like that? He loses so much blood!" she scolded the father.

Phillips was contrite. "I thought it'd be best to let the blood come and wash out the baccy."

"Tobacco?" Abbie asked.

Angeline had brought a basin of water and Abbie was gently washing the wound. Very carefully she lifted the severed tip and set it in place. The blood was coming less forcibly now, but it was still coming. How to stop it? And how to keep the tip in place?

Suddenly she remembered that when Jeffrey Corey had cut his finger his mother had bound it up with brown paper.

"Angeline! Bring me some of that paper Catherine's been saving. In the kitchen cupboard. Hurry, please!"

When the paper was brought she said, "Stop crying, Tommy! Hold this finger tip in place with your left hand. There!" She tore strips of the brown paper and wrapped the finger securely, up and over and around, up and over and around.

"I don't know what else to do, but this should hold it till the doctor comes." She glanced up at the boy's father. "What were you saying about tobacco?"

"Well, you know that cigar cutter I have in the store? You stick the end of a cigar in and a knife clips it off. When this happens, the little man on top takes his cigar out of his mouth. It's just a little iron figure of a man, you understand. I just got the gadget a few days ago."

"I haven't seen yours, Mr. Phillips, but I've seen similar objects in Boston. But what happened?"

"Tommy, here, wanted to show his sister how the thing works, so he stuck in his finger, and wham! the end was cut off, just like the tip of a cigar—"

"Jennie saw how it works, though!" Tommy put in, sniffling.

"That wasn't very smart, Tommy. Now come and lie down—I'll fix it so your hand is kept up, so the blood won't come so fast. I think you could go, Mr. Phillips, if you'll leave Tommy here. Dr. Maynard should be back soon and he'll look at the finger and tell me whether I've done right."

"Well, thank you, Miss Abbie. It sure is a comfort to have someone here when the doc's gone. The bleeding's almost stopped. Now, Tommy, you do exactly what Miss Abbie says!"

Abbie took the boy into one of the empty rooms and had him lie down on the cot there. She removed his shoes, propped the injured hand up on a stack of pillows, and said, "You lie quiet till Dr. Maynard comes home!"

She told Angeline to take the boy a cup of warm milk, and hurried in to look at Mrs. Ebey. The woman lay in deep sleep, but her pulse was about normal, Abbie thought.

"Oh!" she sighed. "I do hope nothing else happens before the Maynards return."

When they did come, they found Abbie bent over the kitchen stove, preparing some beef broth for her patients. She dropped the spoon and turned to her friends.

"Did the baby come? How's Mrs. Blackwell? Was it a boy or a girl? And, oh! you don't know what's been going on here! Mrs. Ebey had some sort of fit—I don't know what it was. And Tommy Phillips cut off his finger. I've been so scared!"

"Whoa, there, girl!" Dr. Maynard took her fluttering hands and held them firmly. "Just tell me what really happened."

Abbie swiftly outlined what had taken place and what she had done. She and Catherine followed him into the bedroom and watched while he examined the woman. He turned around, smiling.

"I suppose she had an epileptic seizure," he said. "She's had them before, but I had no premonition that one would take place while I was gone."

"Is she all right?" Abbie asked fearfully.

"Right as can be expected. You did exactly what you should do in such a case. I could have done no better. All she needs now is rest and some of that beef broth when she wakes. How did you know about putting a roll of cloth in her mouth?"

"I didn't know, but I couldn't stand there and watch her chew her tongue to bits!"

"Well, you're a natural-born nurse, I guess! Now let's look at Tommy."

As they went to the second sickroom Catherine said, "Mrs. Blackwell has a beautiful baby girl and she's doing fine, Abbie. I'm sorry you've had such a hectic morning here alone."

"I'd have died if it hadn't been that Angeline returned. She wouldn't touch Mrs. Ebey, but she did help."

"The Indians think epileptics have been seized by evil spirits, and that it is dangerous to touch them during a convulsion."

Dr. Maynard also approved of Abbie's treatment of the mutilated finger.

"The boy's in fine shape, physically. He'll get along all right, and I wouldn't be at all surprised if that tip grew right back on. I'll take off the brown paper in a little while and see whether it needs stitching. But I'd prefer to just let it heal without that if it will."

That afternoon Dr. Maynard called Abbie into the little cubbyhole that served as his office.

"You've been here a month, Abbie. And it's time you received your first month's salary. It's nowhere near what you have been worth to us, child, but it's a fair share, I think, of what we've taken in this past month." He laid three shiny five-dollar gold pieces on his desk in front of her.

Abbie stared at the glittering coins. "Fifteen dollars! I haven't had that much money ever before! Oh, I'll take it right down to Asa Mercer. Every bit of it!"

Suddenly the thought of that debt to Mercer, of the needlessness of it when fares had been provided for some who could not pay, of her humiliation as a stowaway, all this piled on top of the anxiety and effort of the morning plus the sight of so much money overcame her. She dropped into a chair, covered her face with her hands and wept. Dr. Maynard was amazed.

"Why, what's wrong, child? What on earth? This morning has been too much for you, that's it!"

Abbie struggled for control. "That's not all of it, Dr. Maynard," she said. And then she told him what had been gnawing at her consciousness ever since Seattle's funeral.

"You see where all this puts me? Between Asa Mercer and Tolley Heaton. Mercer has my note for three hundred dollars and Tolley thinks he's paid for me—"

Dr. Maynard shook his head. "You've got it all wrong, Abbie. I guess Tolley didn't explain things very well, and maybe he is a bit confused in his own mind about this project of Asa Mercer's. He did contribute, and so did many others. But it was not as the purchase price on

a bride—it was an investment to help the Territory. If
Asa hadn't had to stay in the East so long; if President
Lincoln hadn't been assassinated and Asa could have got
a ship from him as he planned—Asa knew Lincoln. Did
you know that, Abbie? He sat on his knee and listened
to his stories when he was a little tyke. Well, we all
thought Asa had a wonderful idea, an idea that would be
of great benefit to Washington Territory. But Asa didn't
have the capital to carry out his scheme, so we all chipped
in—"

"We?" Abbie repeated. "You—?"

"Of course I contributed. And I wasn't expecting any
bride, either! We did think that if Asa got five hundred
women, most of whom could pay their passage money,
and then filled the hold of the ship with plows and
lanterns and all sorts of things needed out here, why we'd
make a profit. It didn't work out that way, though. Asa
lost more than any of us. But we still feel that we have
received good value for our investment. The girls and
women Asa brought have entered right into the life of
the settlement and are doing valiant service. Look at
you yourself. Why, just in this one day you've proved
your worth to the town!"

Abbie smiled tremulously. "Then I don't have to—
I'm not sort of obligated to marry someone who's put
money into the venture?"

"Why, of course not! And if your note to Mercer is
troubling you, child, why, maybe I can speak to him."

Abbie's shoulders straightened. "No! Don't do that.
I'll pay my way. I want to, Dr. Maynard. I stowed away

knowing full well that I was obligating myself for the voyage." She stood up, picked up the gold pieces and smiled. "I'm glad I can start paying right away."

"If you'll let me make a suggestion," the doctor said gently, "don't give Mercer your entire wage. Keep back a little—one of those coins, perhaps,—in case you want some money for something."

Abbie hesitated, looking at the glittering coins. Then she made up her mind.

"If you can change one of these, I'll pay Mercer thirteen dollars. Two will be ample for me for the next month."

Dr. Maynard smiled. "That's cutting it close, child. But here you are!" He took five silver dollars from his desk and gave them to her in exchange for the gold piece.

"I'll go down town as soon as I can change my dress— that is, if you don't need me here—"

"No, all's quiet here. Take your time, child!"

Abbie stepped lightly along the path down the hill. She was wearing her lilac-sprigged dimity, with a little lavender parasol over her shoulder as a shield against the afternoon sun. The parasol had been a special gift from Maggie Corey last summer. The sight of it brought back the familiar faces in the widow's cottage. Her heart constricted with longing to see them all again. She had sent a letter out with Roger Conant, but she must get another one ready for the next ship. And a bear claw for Jeff, and maybe an Indian cornhusk doll for Chrissie.

She was glad to have her doubts about Asa Mercer dispelled. Now she understood a little better the complexity

of the project into which she had hurled herself with so
little understanding of all that was involved. No wonder
the newspapers back East had misunderstood Mercer and
his idea. Like herself, they had interpreted the whole
thing from just one crooked angle.

In this mellow mood she found Asa Mercer more
pleasant and more attractive than she had been imagin-
ing him. He asked about her work at the hospital and
chatted about some of the other passengers. As he handed
her a receipt for the thirteen dollars he said in a kindly
tone, "I imagine this is about all you've earned this past
month, Miss Abbie. I hope you aren't cutting yourself
too short in funds."

Abbie murmured, "No. It's all right."

"Even so," Mercer went on, "it's going to take you a
long time to discharge this obligation. And a lot of hard
work. Have you considered that you might accomplish
the same end far more easily?"

Abbie's chin jutted. "By marrying Tolley Heaton? Oh,
I am aware that he thinks he has paid for me. But Dr.
Maynard assures me that such a proposal was not a vital
part of anyone's investment. If Tolley Heaton thinks it
was, he must get his money back some other way!"

Mercer shook his head. "You do get riled so easy, Miss
Abbie. No one's getting his money back—it's all gone—
to pay Holladay, to provide food for the ships, to pay the
board and room back East and in San Francisco—not just
for me, but for my passengers, too." He looked at Abbie
meaningfully. Then he went on quietly, "No. Everyone
who supported the project has lost money. Except the

women and girls themselves. I can say with pride that every one of them has received full value for every cent she has paid."

Abbie was contrite. "Yes, I know that. I'm sorry I spoke hastily."

"But Tolley Heaton, to get back to him, is a very well-to-do man. His eye was caught by you from the very first, Miss Abbie. He would be glad to pay off your note—"

"No, thank you!" Abbie snapped. "I'll pay off my own debt!" Her cheeks burned. How this man could vex her! She caught her lip between her teeth for a moment and then went on more calmly. "I know it will take a long time and a lot of hard work, as you say, Mr. Mercer. But I will pay it off as fast as ever I can. Good day, sir!" She turned with a swish of ruffled petticoats and flounced out of the house and down the dusty path.

As she neared Phillips' store Mrs. Wright and Sybil came around the corner. Abbie forgot her problems and ran forward to greet her friends.

"Sybil! Mrs. Wright! What good luck brings you to town? Were you coming up to the Maynards'? You surely wouldn't leave without coming to see me?"

"Of course not, my dear!" Mrs. Wright said, beaming at Abbie. "We have news for you, Abbie! We're going to be in town now permanently, I think."

"Mamma! Let me tell her, please! Abbie, Mamma's rented that empty building back of the store. She's going to start a bakery. Mr. Cushing is lending her the money and Captain Finch is going to bring up supplies on the *Eliza Anderson* this very next trip!"

"How wonderful!" Abbie exclaimed. "But where'll you live? Hortense is out so far—"

"We'll live right back of the shop. There are rooms which we'll fix up," Mrs. Wright answered. "We just couldn't stay on at Hortense's, doing nothing. And a bakery is needed here. The Continental Hotel and Madame Damnable have both promised to buy their bread and cakes from me."

"Madame Damnable!" Sybil giggled. "You wouldn't think anyone would want to lodge in a place owned by someone called that. But they do! And Captain Finch says every ship that stops here will be glad to get fresh bread."

"I'm sure they will. And I'm so glad you'll be close. Now I can see you almost every day—"

"You won't be the only working girl now, Abbie! I'm going to help Mamma, of course. And besides that, I'm to have the job of delivering the bread. Especially to the ships!" she ended, dimpling with mischief.

Abbie chuckled and gave her friend a hug. "Oh, Sybil, you're incorrigible. Last time I saw you you were in mourning for Rod. Now you're planning on using your charms to captivate some innocent ship's officer!"

"Well," Sybil pouted, "Rod's far, far away and that Phil Strang that's always hanging about is so dull! A girl must have something to look forward to!"

"I'm looking forward to the change, too," Mrs. Wright said soberly. "I came to Seattle to make a new life for myself, and this seems to be my chance. I couldn't do it, of course, without the help of Mr. Cushing. He's to be a partner and will share in the profits. And there should be profits if we work hard."

"It will be more exciting, I guess," Abbie said. "Catherine Maynard says that as soon as the heat breaks there'll be all sorts of amusements—lectures, amateur theatricals, socials— Oh, this makes my day perfect. And something was needed to do that!"

Laughing a bit, she related the events of her morning, and of her encounter with Mercer.

Mrs. Wright patted Abbie's arm in a gesture of tolerant understanding. "You've been touchy with Mr. Mercer ever since he found you in the sewing closet!" she said gently. "I can see why, too. He shouldn't have dragged you out the way he did. But then he was upset—he's as emotional and mercurial a man as I've ever met. But I sincerely like and admire him."

"Oh, so do I," Abbie agreed, but not too enthusiastically.

# 9 ←←←←←←←←←←←←←←←←←←←←←←←←←←←←←

IN JULY THE RAINS CAME, WARM, MISTY rains that did little to break the heat. The forest and the verges of the streams steamed. The dusty streets were changed into quagmires, ankle deep in sticky mud. Abbie stood at the window of the Maynards' front room and stared out at the vaporous landscape.

"It's like the jungle," she murmured. "No wonder everything is so green and luxuriant."

Catherine Maynard came and stood beside her. "This has been an unusual summer—the hottest anyone remembers. And now these rains. Oh, we always have rain, but not like this—so terribly warm."

Abbie turned from the window. "I thought I'd go down and see Sybil, since we're not busy just now. But I'm afraid I could never make it through that gumbo."

"Gumbo?"

"That's what they used to call mud on the prairie. I always thought it was such an expressive word."

Mrs. Maynard, still looking out of the window, said, "Maybe it's just as well that the gumbo kept you here. If I'm not mistaken, someone is coming to see you."

Abbie peeked over the woman's shoulder. Worth

Barton was plowing his way up the path. He was rain-soaked and mud-splashed and looked very disreputable. Abbie giggled nervously.

"If his high-toned New York friends could only see him now!" she murmured.

Worth came up onto the wide porch. He took off his hat and shook the rain from the brim. Then, very calmly, he hooked his boot heel over a projecting edge of floor board and yanked off the mud-caked item. He removed the other boot in the same way, stood both neatly against the wall, and in his heavily stockinged feet knocked on the door.

Catherine Maynard opened it and greeted him warmly. She knew him, as the Maynards knew everyone. At her invitation he came into the room, making no apology for his unshod feet. He saw Abbie and went straight to her.

"Hello, sweetheart!" he said happily. "Here I am! Came to town just so's I could take you to Asa's wedding tomorrow."

Abbie felt laughter bubbling up in her. She was unaccountably happy. But some silly perversity made her say, "Let me think! I can't seem to remember but what I've already promised—"

Worth took her shoulders between his two strong hands. "I don't care if you've promised, or whom you've promised. I've come in this miserable rain to take you to the wedding, and take you I shall."

Abbie motioned toward the windowpanes, streaming with rain. "Despite the weather I've found a sort of paradise here—as Asa Mercer said once, 'an Eden without Eves.' But oh, what Adams!"

"I know!" Worth said, his bantering tone changing. "I know that one particular Adam has been hanging around you all the time I've been out in the lonely wilderness, hunting for coal, trying to make a stake so that we'll have something to start out on. Abbie, darling!" his arm about her shoulders drew her close and he bent to kiss the tip of her ear, showing under the golden curls. "I'm envious. Envious of Asa Mercer and his Annie!"

Abbie relaxed for a moment in his arms. It was so good to feel them about her. Such a comfort and joy. Then she drew away.

"Isn't it wonderful?" she said brightly. "Annie's had her eye on him since the day she boarded the *Continental*. And now that they're actually getting married, he'll feel that he has indeed been repaid for his suffering last summer." She grew serious. "But Worth, while you've been gone Tolley Heaton has been very good—"

"Don't tell me!" Worth groaned. "Don't tell me!"

"He'll be expecting to take me to the wedding. And I am sure he's been invited." It was a sly reference to Worth's treatment at that first party, when he had been a sort of interloper.

"I've been invited, too!" he said with dignity. "In fact, word went out that *everyone* was invited. I was invited, specially, to some of the other weddings that have been taking place—Sarah Ann Robinson sent an Indian messenger to urge me to come when she married Dave Webster. That was just a few days after I left for Black River.

And Mrs. Wakeman and Mrs. Peterson. She got a husband even with those obstreperous children of hers. Oh,
I haven't been forgotten, my love."

"But you didn't come to any of those! You didn't care
enough—I had to go alone or with Tolley!" Abbie said
slowly. "It would only be fair—"

Worth took her by the shoulders and shook her gently.
"I can just see the thoughts chasing around in that pretty,
golden head of yours. Like little mice trying to find a
way out. But you might as well give up, Abbie, my girl.
You are going to this particular wedding with me. Everyone on the ship knew that you were my girl and they'll
all be at Mercer's party. I'm not going to let them get
the idea that I've been cut out by any lumberjack. And
I'm not going to let you get that idea, either. The fun
starts at six, so be ready."

He kissed her again, this time soundly on the lips.
Then he let her go and stomped to the door, his stomps
deadened by his stockinged feet. Abbie wanted to cry
out, "Worth! Worth! Of course I'm your girl! Come
back and kiss me again!" But that would never do. He
was too sure of her already.

She was glad that there were only two patients in the
hospital, neither of them seriously ill. One was a sailor,
almost recovered from a broken ankle he got when he
tried to jump from the deck of the *Eliza Anderson* to
the dock without benefit of gangway. The other was an
Indian, suffering from burns he received when he held a
firecracker in his hand during the Fourth of July celebration.

She climbed the ladder to her attic and took from its

hook her lilac-sprigged dimity. She studied it critically.
"Dearie me!" she sighed, frowning. "Worth will be so
tired of seeing me in this dress. I had to wear it for every
good time on the ship. It's lucky the material has stood
all it's gone through!"

Tucking the gown under her arm she scurried down
to the kitchen and set to work. The ruching at collar and
wrist was limp and frayed. She carefully removed it,
mended it, and then gently washed the fragile material.
Before it was dry she dipped it in sugar water to stiffen
it, and pressed it while it was still damp, carefully pleat-
ing it into a ruche. She wished she had Maggie Corey's
crimping iron, it would do the work so much more
quickly and evenly.

She was hard at work over the sadiron, the steaming
heat curling her hair in dark little tendrils on her brow,
when Catherine Maynard called her into the front room.
Tolley Heaton was there.

"Howdy, Miss Abbie!" he greeted her. He was always
a little bashful at first, but he soon grew easier in Abbie's
friendly company.

Abbie smiled and invited him to be seated. They
chatted for a moment or two. Then the young man came
to the purpose of his visit, which Abbie had already
guessed.

"I reckon you'd want to go to Asa's wedding tomorrow,
so I came over to tell you I'd be around for you, if you
don't mind."

"Oh, Tolley!" Abbie felt genuinely sorry for him. "I'm
sorry, but I've already promised Worth Barton that I'd
go with him." She saw the look of surprise and hurt on

Tolley's expressive face and felt that some explanation was due. "He came in from wherever he's been on purpose to take me. He knows all the girls who will be there. It will be a sort of get-together for all of us who were on the *Continental*. I couldn't refuse—"

"No. I suppose not," Tolley muttered.

A sudden thought struck her. "Look, Tolley, why don't you ask Sybil to go with you? I'll wager she'll be glad to—"

"But what about Phil?"

"Bother Phil! Sybil doesn't care for him, and she thinks you are far more fun than he. She's told me so. You like Sybil, don't you?"

"Yes, I like her," Tolley admitted. "She's a pretty little trick and full of fun." He considered a moment. "You'll dance with me some?" he asked.

"Of course I will, Tolley. I love to dance with you."

"Do you think Sybil really will go with me?" he asked doubtfully.

"Of course, if you get there before Phil does. But if she's already promised she can't break her word, any more than I can, so you better hurry—"

He rose to go, but gave her a penetrating look. "See here now, Miss Abbie. Just because I take Sybil this time, don't get the notion that I don't want to squire you around. Next party that comes, I want to take you. I'm speaking now so I'll be sure to be first."

The next day was bright and clear, but the sun just did not have time enough to dry up the mud. This posed problems for the crowds making their way toward Yesler's Hall. The women and girls stepped along carefully, hold-

ing high their skirts and petticoats, carrying their slippers
and placing their boot-shod feet gingerly to avoid muddy-
ing their flounces. Even the men walked gingerly, but
every now and then a screech would betray someone
who had clumsily plumped down a big foot and splashed
mud on his partner.

As Abbie had anticipated, everyone was attending the
event—all the settlers, who held Asa Mercer in high
esteem, and all the passengers who had watched the ro-
mance blossom on the *Continental*.

In front of the hall the men scraped mud from their
shoes, scrubbed them against the grass, and tried to make
their footwear presentable on the dance floor, for of
course there would be dancing after the supper. Mean-
while, in the small room reserved as a dressing room for
the ladies, the female contingent removed their muddy
boots and donned their party slippers. When Abbie was
ready she stepped out to find Worth waiting for her.

"Prettiest girl in the whole shebang!" he said proudly.

"Oh, Worth, I'm afraid you're mighty tired of seeing
me in this dress. But it's all I have—"

Worth grinned. "I love it. When we're married I'll
have it framed to hang on the cabin wall where I can
gaze at it and think about our courtship days."

"Courtship?" Abbie said with a little scornful laugh.
"What courtship? Oh, you were attentive enough on the
ship, I'll admit. But you were always joking—and since
we've been here I've scarcely seen you. And when I have
seen you, you have—"

"Let you know that you're my girl."

"Yes. Or at least tried to. But you sort of overlooked

the courtship part, didn't you? I thought courtship meant—"

"It means just this," Worth said, and before the gaping crowd he picked her up off her feet and gave her a resounding kiss. "Now, that's what I call courtship!" he said, putting her down.

Someone guffawed and Abbie felt her face flaming. Why did Worth have to do things like that? She turned away, angry and embarrassed, but Worth took her arm and said, grinning, "There's Sybil. Looks as if she's stepping into your discarded shoes. Let's join them."

Abbie went along quietly. She didn't dare answer him because she had no idea how he would react to anything she said. And she didn't want a scene; she didn't want to be embarrassed again.

The long tables had already been set for the wedding supper. As was the custom, the older women of the town were bustling about, placing platters and baskets and bowls of food everywhere. Abbie had marveled every time she had attended one of these frontier socials. No matter how many came, there was enough food for all.

"It's like the Indian potlatch," Tolley had told her. "Everyone brings something, and it seems to sort of multiply as it's passed around."

Asa Mercer and Annie had been married earlier in the day by the Reverend Daniel Bagley. It had been a simple ceremony at the little white Methodist Protestant church on the hillside. Now the couple stood near the door with Asa's brother Thomas and his wife Hester, greeting the guests.

Abbie kissed Annie, murmuring, "We knew this was

going to happen from the time we left New York. He adores you, Annie. How happy you both must be."

Annie gave her an answering hug. "You'll be next, Abbie!"

Abbie's eyes darkened. How could Annie say that when she knew that her husband held that note for three hundred dollars! Did Annie think she was going to get married to have someone cancel her debt? If so, she was wrong! Very wrong.

Abbie was glad this polite duty was over. She wanted to get to Sybil, who was wearing an elegant new dress of soft pink muslin, in which her dark prettiness glowed vividly. She reminded Abbie of the sweetbrier roses that grew so profusely around the cottages.

"Wherever did you get it, Sybil? It's perfectly lovely!"

Sybil sparkled. "Rod sent it—and a long, sweet letter. He was held up in San Francisco for more than a month, waiting for a ship to take him back to New York. And before he left he wrote all about what had been happening down there, and got this dress. Captain Finch brought it—just yesterday." She held out the soft, rosy skirt and pirouetted.

"It's lovely!" Abbie repeated sincerely.

"I'm so glad Tolley asked me to come with him. It's too nice a dress to waste on Phil—he never sees what I wear, anyway. But Tolley did. He's been very nice."

Abbie laughed. "It's certainly no fun having a new dress that isn't noticed. But yours is, you may be sure. Just look at the envious glances you're getting!"

"You don't mind my coming with Tolley?" Sybil whispered.

"Of course not, darling. I had to accept Worth's invitation when he was in town."

"I know," Sybil said slowly. "Tolley told me he asked you first. He is so distractingly honest! But I'm glad he likes me well enough to come to me when you fail him!"

"Where's your mother?" Abbie asked. "Let's find places by her."

"And Dell Cushing and Hortense and John. They are all together. Over there!"

The quartet of young friends made their way down the hall and found seats across from the others. Abbie's eyes studied Hortense, and suddenly she smiled. She leaned across Worth and whispered something to Sybil. It would be improper for the men to hear what she asked. Sybil laughed and nodded.

"That's wonderful!" Abbie cried. Mrs. Wright beamed, understanding what the girls were whispering about. Hortense smiled smugly.

This wedding outshone those that had gone before. There was more food, more music, more gaiety.

"Of course!" Sybil said when Abbie mentioned this. "Asa Mercer is one of the shining lights of Seattle. His brother is very well-to-do, and Annie Stephens isn't lacking in money, I know. Her clothes gave that away when she boarded the *Continental*. But she was a war orphan and so entitled to come if she wanted to."

"Mercer's Belles are doing all right for themselves," Worth remarked teasingly. He leaned over and whispered in Sybil's ear. "What about a certain nice Boston lady not far from us?" He winked.

Sybil said thoughtfully, "You're probably right. It

would be wonderful for Mamma. Dell's very good to her and I like him a lot."

"Well!" Abbie interrupted, "everyone hasn't been looking for a husband. Carrie Bacon and Grace Loring are going to teach the smaller children here in Seattle this winter. Annie Connor is going to teach at Olympia and Clara Lord has been offered a position in the Steilacoom school and Mrs. Osborne's teaching at Tumwater. Asa Mercer said they needed teachers out here, and I think most of the passengers came in good faith to meet that—or some other need."

She had spoken more earnestly than seemed necessary, and Worth laughed.

Tolley said soberly, "We need wives worse than we need teachers. If we don't have wives, pretty soon there won't be any children to teach."

Sybil giggled and Worth chuckled. "Right you are, sir!" he said. "And take my word for it, most of these women and girls came out, in very good faith, to meet that need."

"You're horrible!" Abbie cried. "Absolutely horrible!"

At the other end of the hall the musicians were tuning up their instruments. Worth took Abbie's hand and drew her to her feet.

"But a very good dancer!" he said. "Come on, it's my favorite quadrille, and we have just enough for a set all our own!"

Sam Benson, caller for all the dances, stepped up on a chair. Asa and his bride stepped out to form the head set as Sam called out,

"Hurry, folks, fill the hall!
Get your partners, one and all.
Find your honey, find your sweet,
Get that gal out on her feet!"

Laughing, Dell Cushing and Mrs. Wright came to face Abbie and Worth. The others joined them to form a square. Worth began to sing,

"Swing your gal just as you please,
Make her show her dimpled knees."

Worth picked Abbie up and swung her around, not waiting for the caller's singsong directions. Everyone laughed. Then Sam's voice demanded attention and the dance really began.

# 10 ‹‹‹‹‹‹‹‹‹‹‹‹‹‹‹‹‹‹‹‹‹‹‹‹‹‹‹‹‹‹‹

"It's such a lovely night!" Worth said as he and Abbie came up onto the Maynards' front porch that evening after the wedding. "Let's not waste it, Abbie, darling. Let's sit here awhile and just drink it in."

He pulled her down beside him on the top step, put his arm around her and drew her close. For some minutes they sat like this, looking out over the Sound. The air was clean and fresh-smelling and softly warm. Abbie was filled with such peace and contentment as she had never before known.

At last Worth said softly, "This wedding fever is contagious. I've caught it, Abbie. Let's get married. Now! Before I go back up the river."

Abbie spoke softly. "You know I can't, Worth. Not until I've paid off my note to Asa Mercer."

"Oh, forget Mercer and that confounded note! Why should they stand in our way? I love you and you love me and that's all that counts."

Abbie was still tranquil. Just to hear what Worth would say, she asked, "How do you know I love you? You've never asked me. And you've never really told me that you love me, either. Not seriously—you've just joked about it—"

121

"I'm telling you now, darling. And as for your telling me, your eyes, your smiles, your blushes have told me for a long, long time."

Surprised, Abbie drew away. "I wasn't aware of it!" she said primly.

"Oh, I think you were, my dear. And don't get uppity with me tonight, sweetheart. It's just too nice an evening to be spoiled. Let's talk about our wedding."

"There's no use to talk about that yet. It will be a long, long time before I can even think about it. I still owe Mercer two hundred and eighty-seven dollars! Oh, Worth, it's a tremendous debt! And at the rate the Maynards can pay me—I don't know when I'll get it off my shoulders."

"Well, marry me and I'll pay Mercer. I just can't bear to go off again and leave you here. When I think how that Tolley Heaton looks at you and how gay you are when you dance with him—well, I just want you safely my wife. That's all."

"It sounds as if you don't trust me!"

"I don't trust that good-looking Tolley Heaton. He'd just as lief steal my girl as not. In fact, he'd rather steal her."

His bantering tone changed to seriousness. "All nonsense aside, my darling, why should we wait?"

"I've told you," Abbie answered patiently. "I do not want to bring a horrible debt as my dowry. It's bad enough to come to you penniless, with no trousseau, hardly any clothes. But I won't add a debt that I incurred myself and that I am determined to pay by myself. And besides, you said that you'd just caught the fever. You may get over it, who knows?"

"You know I didn't mean that! Abbie, are you going to wreck our happiness over a miserable note?" His voice betrayed his irritation.

"If it can be wrecked so easily," Abbie said sadly, "it is not worth much. Oh, I wish you could understand! I wish you could see how I feel! I've never owed anyone a cent before. I've never been beholden to anyone. I've tried to pay my way. Oh, I owe Maggie Corey a great deal—I know that and it bothers me, too. But that's different—it's not money—money that I promised I'd pay." Her chin jutted in its childishly stubborn way. "And I will pay it, too. Nothing can stop me."

"Well," Worth said coldly, "I've learned long ago that when your chin gets set there's no use pleading with you." He got to his feet. Abbie stood up, too. "So I might as well bid you good night, Miss Cabot, and wish you financial success! If that's the only kind you want!" He ended bitterly.

Abbie put her hands on his arm. Her lips were trembling.

"Don't go away angry, Worth, please!" she pleaded. "You haven't really asked me, but I'll tell you. I do love you—I love you very much!"

He took her in his arms and kissed her. "Abbie, Abbie!" he whispered. "Say you'll marry me. Now!"

"No, Worth, not now. But sometime—if you'll wait."

He dropped his arms and turned away. "I don't know what I'll do!" he muttered, and went down the steps and off into the darkness.

For a long time Abbie couldn't get to sleep. She lay turning over and over in her mind wild schemes for getting money to pay Mercer. At thirteen dollars a month —even if she were paid that much every month—it would take her nearly two years! Would Worth wait that long?

But what could she do? She had thought of getting a position as a schoolteacher. They were paid as much as thirty and forty dollars a month. But when she had made inquiries she found that older women or girls who had had some experience in the schools back home had been chosen for every available place. Maybe she had been hasty in grasping this job at the hospital. But she had thought it wise to get something immediately—and even the schoolteaching pay wouldn't start till fall. The whole summer gone!

She awakened with a dull, depressed feeling, her nerves on edge. However, her personal worries were soon swamped in the daily routine of bathing and feeding the two patients, airing the rooms, changing the bedding, washing and ironing and cooking. She worked without enthusiasm, her earlier zeal dulled by the monotony of unimaginative, repeated chores. Worth did not come by, but from the front porch she saw him and his Indian workers go past the foot of the hill and into the forest. He was off again on his explorations of the Black River area in search of coal.

Abbie never knew how it happened, but one morning she awakened with a full-blown plan in mind. As soon as her routine jobs were finished, she asked Catherine if she could go down into town. The doctor's wife smilingly gave the desired permission.

Abbie brushed her curls carefully, donned her modest brown bombazine, and departed down the hill toward the main street where most of the business houses stood. She went straight to Dan Phillips' store on the corner of First and Washington. Just around the corner, snuggled up against the larger building, was the small shop where Sybil's mother had her bakery.

A cluster of Indians lounged on the wide porch in front of the store. Abbie had grown used to these knots of silent, immovable figures, but at first the knowledge that the dark, inscrutable eyes were following her every movement on the street had somewhat disconcerted her. Now, lifting her skirts as she stepped across outflung legs, she entered the store.

It was rather dark inside, and she peered about trying to locate the owner. He was nowhere in sight. At the long counter down one side of the store, Mrs. Phillips was waiting on a customer. She had a baby in one arm and a small child was tugging at her apron. The customer was Madame Damnable, owner of one of the town's most popular lodginghouses. A group of lumberjacks were trying on plaid shirts, with plenty of horseplay and rough jokes to enliven their efforts. In one corner, an Indian woman sat on the floor, trying to sew a button on a shirt, while a tough-looking young fellow stood over her, trying to hurry her along. Abbie saw a chance to make herself useful.

She went to the Indian and with a smile and a kind word, which she hoped the woman would understand, she gently took the garment from the bungling hands and with swift, deft strokes sewed the button firmly in place.

"Thank 'e, miss," the young man said as he took the shirt. "Ain't you one of them females Asa Mercer brought to town? Yes! I'm sartin I saw you when the sloop docked. And be ye spoken for yet? I could make danged good use of a pretty little wench that's handy like you be."

Abbie flushed and shook her head. "You've no right—" she began indignantly, but he interrupted.

"No call to git uppity, miss. It's a right honorable offer I was making. I didn't have no three hundred dollars to bribe that feller to pick out a gal fer me, but if there's one about that ain't being picked up, I'd gladly oblige."

"No, I thank you!" Abbie said shortly and turned away. She didn't want him to see the amusement in her eyes, he was so obviously in earnest.

As she turned, her eyes met those of Dan Phillips. He had come through the back doorway, and was watching her with a wide, good-natured grin.

"You can't say you never had an offer, Miss Abbie," he chortled. "Take your shirt, Les, and I'll take your money."

As soon as the fellow had paid and left the store, Dan Phillips turned to Abbie. "What can I do for you, now?"

Abbie spoke in a low voice, hoping she would not be overheard.

"I'll tell you, Mr. Phillips. I've just got to earn more money than I can get at the hospital. I owe Mr. Mercer for my passage out here, and I want to pay him off as fast as I can."

"He isn't nagging you for it, is he?" Phillips asked. "He shouldn't worry you—"

"No, it isn't that. It's just that I want to get the note paid and out of the way. Dr. Maynard pays me as much as he can, but you know how it is—the Indians and even some of the settlers just don't pay. They want help immediately when they're sick or hurt, but after they get well, they let things slide."

Phillips nodded. "Same trouble here," he muttered. Then he looked shrewdly at Abbie. "You asking me for a job, Miss Abbie? I doubt I could pay even as much as the doc."

"Not a job, exactly. It's like this. I've been wondering what I could do—something I could build into a real little business. Mrs. Wright's started a bakery; Mrs. Larson has a laundry; and the Burke sisters have opened a millinery shop. Well, I am not talented along any such lines. But I had an idea." She paused for breath and Phillips said, "Go on, Miss Abbie!"

"Well, many of the people that have come to the hospital have asked me to write letters for them. I did it willingly, of course, and didn't charge them anything. But I got to thinking that there must be a lot of folks out here who would like help in writing letters. So I thought if I could just have a desk down in town here, some place where people came, I could offer such a service and charge a little for it—"

Phillips chewed on the end of his mustache. "It's an idea all right, Miss Abbie. But where do I come in?"

Now, fully launched, Abbie's words came swiftly, easily. She explained that she hoped the store owner would let her have room for a small table or desk and put a sign in his window telling about her service. That was all she wanted. She could not afford to pay for this accommodation in money, but she would pay for it by helping out in the store when she was not busy writing.

"You do need help—better than that squaw you have. I suppose many garments arrive with buttons off, or loose —or with tears in them. The last sack of flour Mrs. Maynard bought had a great rent in the end—she was pretty angry at losing so much of the stuff. I'd keep a needle and thread handy and when I had a minute I'd mend things for you, or wait on customers. I think this would amount to fair pay for the little room I'd be taking."

Phillips regarded her quizzically. "You'd be a sort of drawing card yourself, I reckon. A pretty girl like you sitting in the store! All the bachelors in the Territory would be finding they needed something. Joe Williamson would turn green with envy. And Charlie Plummer, too! Wouldn't surprise me if I put them about out of business. Yes, siree! It sounds pretty good. But of course we haven't any idea whether you'd get any customers yourself. That's something that has never been tried here—"

"Oh, I'm sure I'll have customers! Why, some of the fellows the doctor has treated can't even read or write. Yet they must have friends they'd like to send a letter to."

"We can try it—say, for a month, maybe."

Abbie shook her head. "It might take a month for the word to get around. And I wouldn't want to quit my sure job at the hospital unless you'd let me stay until I proved to be a failure."

"You're a pretty shrewd worker, Miss Abbie. Well, I'm sort of a gambler at heart. I'll agree to your plan if you'll promise that if you've not made a go of it by the end of the year, you'll quit without any to-do."

"Oh, thank you! That's fair enough! I do thank you, Mr. Phillips."

"Well, now, no need to thank me. I ought to be willing to give you a chance after the way you fixed up Tommy's finger."

"It's all right, I know. I was glad to do what I could."

"Yep! It's about as good as new. Just a slight scar there —a good thing! May remind him to keep his fingers out of things!" They laughed together. "When do you want to start?" Phillips asked.

"Monday, I think. I'll have to tell the Maynards and maybe help train someone to do what I've been doing. Princess Angeline's niece has been hanging about the place. Maybe she can learn."

The Maynards accepted her planned departure with gracious kindliness.

"I'm sorry I couldn't pay you more, Abbie, child," the doctor said. "But I'd like to suggest this, since you are so eager to get that Mercer debt paid. If we get swamped here—may we call on you, in an emergency, that is? It would be a great comfort to know someone as knowledgeable as you would come when we need help."

"Of course! Oh, that would be wonderful. And this

little business I've told you about won't be so demanding, I'm sure, that I can't pick up and leave at almost any time."

"I'm glad for you, my dear," Catherine said. "Now, when a patient wants letters written we'll send him down to you—providing, of course, that he's a paying patient! Abbie, dear, don't do business on credit. You'll never get ahead if you do!"

"That's a little hardhearted for one in my position," Abbie said with a smile. "I'm doing this just because someone let me use my credit!"

"Where will you live, child?" the doctor asked. "Do you want to keep your room here? It isn't very attractive —and climbing that hill every day may not appeal to you—"

"Oh, Dr. Maynard! I do like my room, and the hill is nothing. But I think I'll try to find a place in town, so I can be more available at all hours. I'll have my desk in the store, but if I can get a room somewhere, I might get some evening jobs, too. I must do everything I can."

"What did Worth think of your plan?" Catherine asked.

"I didn't tell him. I didn't think of it when he was here. I just knew I must do something, and I kept turning ideas over in my head. Then, suddenly, I had this one. I do hope it works!"

Abbie pondered a good deal over what to put on her little sign. Finally she had it:

LETTER WRITING
VERSES FOR ALL OCCASIONS

That last ought to get her some clients, what with all the bachelors hunting for wives. Her first customers were mystified.

"We understand about letters," they said, "but this verse business. What does it mean?"

Abbie explained. A special verse, written for some particular person or occasion, added a great deal to the appeal of a gift. Or a verse could be used in place of a gift. Most women would rather have a verse written just for them than any other kind of present.

"Sort of like a valentine?" one fellow said, grinning. "Valentine's Day all the year long?"

"That's it exactly!" Abbie said enthusiastically.

"What about love letters, miss?" That was Les Crismon, on whose shirt she had sewed the button. "Kin you fix love letters in poetry?"

Abbie's candid gray eyes regarded him. "Yes, sir. If you tell me what you want to say, I'll put it into verse for you."

"Gosh! How'd I know what I want to say? If I knew what to say I could write my own letters. You'd have to figger it out for me. That's what you git paid for, ain't it?"

Abbie suppressed a smile. "I'd do my best, then."

The lumberjack beamed down on her. "Wal, I'll be in fer a pome right soon, you kin bet!"

Abbie was kept busy all that first day. She was surprised at the immediate success of her venture, but cautioned herself that this might not last. Now it was a novelty. There seemed to be a sort of competition among the young men. The older men and the housewives were curious to see what she would turn out for each of their widely varied demands.

She had not revealed her scheme to Sybil and Mrs. Wright. She was afraid they might think she was hinting that they take her into their little house. She was going to stay at the Maynards' until she found the right place to board. But of course she had not been long at her desk when Sybil came bouncing in.

"Oh, Abbie, you rascal! So you've started a business of your own—like a lot of us. How marvelous! And look at the crowd! Well—will you write a letter for me?"

"Of course not!" Abbie said, laughing happily. "You can write your own letters, you goose!"

"But I can't write verse. You know that! You wrote all such assignments for me when we were in school together. So be a darling and write a lovely, lovely poem to thank Rod for my beautiful dress!"

"Later, if you really mean it, Sybil. I think you are just joking."

"I'm not. But have you left the hospital for good, Abbie? What will the Maynards do without you?"

"I'm still living there. And last week I helped Catherine train Angeline's niece—she isn't as smart as her aunt, but she is willing. And I'm still going to help out if they get submerged."

"You can't live away up there on that hill!" Sybil declared. "It's getting late summer. Soon it'll be dark when the store closes. And you traipsing all that way alone. It's impossible. You'll have to move in with us."

Abbie flushed with pleasure, but she demurred. "I don't know. You haven't room for an extra—"

"Extra!" Sybil squealed. "When were you ever an extra?"

Later that day Sybil's mother came in to repeat the invitation and to urge Abbie to accept. "We've missed you more than you know, Abbie. Do come!" She leaned close and said in a low, sober voice, "You'll be doing me a favor, my dear. I'll be frank with you. Mr. Cushing wants to marry me and we'd go down to Olympia for a few days. I'd like to have you with Sybil—"

Abbie impulsively threw her arms about the woman and kissed her. "I'm so happy for you. It's a wonderful idea. And of course I'll come. I can't tell you what this means to me! To be with you folks again! The Maynards have been lovely to me, but you—you seem like family!"

There was some argument about what Abbie should pay. Mrs. Wright contended that she'd be earning her room and board by being a companion to Sybil. But Abbie was determined, and finally a nominal price was set. Abbie happily moved in with her old friends.

Surprisingly, her business continued to flourish and her income soared. She charged only twenty-five cents for an average letter, and from twenty-five cents to a dollar for a set of verses. She refused to call them poems, though most of her customers gave them that dignity. She kept the coins in a tin tobacco jar, and they seemed to multiply out of all reason.

"Just look, Sybil!" she said at the end of the first week, pouring the spate of silver coins out onto the bed she shared with her friend. "Come and help me count it!"

Laughing, they stacked the coins: quarters, fifty-cent pieces, silver dollars.

"Fourteen dollars and seventy-five cents!" she crowed. "Nearly an average of two dollars and a half a day! Oh, Sybil, isn't it wonderful! And it's just been fun, fun, fun! No work at all. Why, at the hospital I worked from daylight till after dark and got only fifteen dollars that first month. And not quite that much the second month, since so many of the patients didn't pay. This isn't all profit, of course. And I will have to spend a little for things I absolutely need. And I can't hope that it will keep up like this. But if I just have half this luck, I'll get Mercer paid off in less than two years! Maybe—oh, I daren't say it—"

"Maybe by next summer!" Sybil said it for her.

Dan Phillips was delighted. His store was always filled, and while Abbie was writing letters her clients did their shopping.

"You're worth a mint of money to me!" he said happily. "And it's doing you good, too, my girl. Golly, but you have gotten prettier and prettier!"

"I like people!" Abbie said. "I just love being with folks. For two years I was starved—and then, up at the hospital I saw people, but I worked awfully hard. This isn't work at all. It's just pleasure."

Mrs. Phillips, nursing her baby, chuckled. "A body can see that it's fun for you, Miss Abbie. And folks like you. Old Man Trowbridge said you could put things down far prettier than he could even think them, let alone write them."

As Catherine Maynard had said, as soon as the heat and the heavy rains were over, the social life picked up. There were more weddings to attend; there were church socials and picnics. Mrs. Chase, one of the *Continental* passengers, started a series of lectures on spiritualism, which most of the young people attended. One group worked up plays and presented them in Yesler's Hall.

"It's a good thing you're not tied down at that hospital!" Sybil said one evening as they waited for Tolley and Phil to escort them to see *The Artful Dodger*. "You'd probably never get away to any of these things!"

"I know," Abbie said slowly. "But sometimes I feel guilty, having so much fun, being so happy. And Worth away off there somewhere, probably lonely—"

"That Worth!" Sybil declared. "He could come to town once in a while if he wanted to. And he could send you a letter. His Indians come in—have to get supplies."

"Yes," Abbie said thoughtfully. She remembered how Worth had told her he'd been invited to the earlier weddings but he hadn't bothered to come in for them. But he was working, not playing. And he was cross with her. His Indians probably reported how she was gallivanting around to all the parties with Tolley Heaton.

"I shouldn't go so often with Tolley," she said slowly.

"You can stop any time you wish!" Sybil said saucily. "I won't let him grieve over it."

"Poor Phil!"

"Poor Phil, nothing! I've told him I can never care for him. I've advised him to go with other girls and, as you very well know, I've often gone with other fellows—especially that handsome Carl Nordstrom, every time the *Eliza Anderson* is in port when there's a party."

Abbie laughed. "You certainly made delivering bread to the ship pay off there! Caught a second mate, no less!"

"The Captain's married as you well know!" Sybil said merrily. "Listen! I hear the boys coming. Into the bedroom! We don't want them to know we were waiting. Mamma—" she called softly.

Mrs. Wright looked in from the kitchen, where she was mixing cookie dough ready for early morning baking.

"Let the boys in—tell them we'll be ready pretty soon!"

Mrs. Wright shook her head reprovingly. But she was smiling as the two girls closed the bedroom door on their giggling.

# 11 ◀◀◀◀◀◀◀◀◀◀◀◀◀◀◀◀◀◀◀◀◀◀◀◀◀◀◀◀◀◀◀

SYBIL'S MOTHER AND DEL CUSHING WERE married on a lovely autumn day.

"The whole world has dressed up in its best for my wedding!" she said, smiling happily. "Look at the sky, the water—the gold and red of the oak and maple against the dark green of the pines! Oh, it's a lovely day, and I am so very happy!"

It was a quiet wedding, with only her family, Abbie and a few other friends attending the simple ceremony performed by the Reverend Daniel Bagley.

Asa Mercer and his bride were present, of course. After he had felicitated the beaming couple he turned to Abbie.

"And when will we be invited to your wedding, Miss Abbie?"

Abbie was too happy, now, too sure of herself to be discomfited by the man's question.

"When I can tear up that note you hold!" she answered, laughing.

The newlyweds went down to Olympia for a week's honeymoon, leaving the bakery in Sybil's charge. Mrs. Parker, one of Mercer's passengers on the *Continental*, had been engaged to come and help each day. One of the obstreperous Peterson youngsters was hired as delivery boy.

Sybil took her responsibilities seriously. She was up long before dawn the day after her mother left. Abbie, awakened by the noise in the kitchen, drew on her dressing gown and went out to see what was going on. Engulfed in a huge apron, Sybil was energetically kneading dough.

"My gracious, Sybil!" Abbie said with a smile. "Did you have to get up by lamplight?"

Sybil looked up. Her dark eyes were shining; her cheek was daubed with flour. "I just want to be sure I get things done on time!" she answered. "Oh, I hope my bread is as good as Mamma's. I don't want to lose any customers!"

Abbie laughed. "It's not likely. You've helped your mother enough to know all about it. You look so happy, Sybil. Do you like being the boss?"

"I'm glad Mamma trusts me enough to leave me in charge," Sybil said honestly. "A year ago she wouldn't have."

"You've grown up a lot in this past year, as we all have, I guess. There's something about being thrown upon the land—having to depend on yourself, on your own resources, that seems to change you. I know I feel ages older than I did when we left Boston." She picked up a small bit of dough and rolled it between her fingers. "This has a fine texture, Sybil," she said encouragingly. Then, "I'll hurry home tonight, if I can be of any help."

She was clearing up her desk, which was really only a

pine table Dan Phillips had lent her, when a familiar voice said, "Don't close up shop yet, miss!"

Her heart leaped; her eyes flew to the dear, so-long-missed face. Worth smiled down at her quizzically.

"I want you to write a letter for me, miss!" he said, pretending not to see the shining light in her eyes, making out that he was a stranger.

"Oh, Worth! You don't mean that! You can very well write your own letters."

"There's a sign in the window that says you write letters, miss. Is it your practice to turn away cash customers?"

"You're just teasing me. How have you been? I'm so—"

"I'm an honest customer and I expect courteous treatment. Now, miss, let's get to work without any more shilly-shallying."

Abbie picked up her pen and said coolly, "Very well, sir. To whom do you wish to address this missive."

Worth flopped down into the client's chair, crossed his long legs and pretended to consider the problem.

"Just start it 'Dear Friend.' At least I'm hoping this person is still a friend. One never can tell, can one? But 'Dear Friend' is sort of harmless and, well, meaningless, isn't it?"

Abbie drew a sheet of paper toward her, dipped her pen in ink and shaped the letters in her neat, precise script.

"Probably you can phrase this better than I can," Worth went on, "since you're a professional letter writer. Just tell this friend—it's a female, by the way—that I have been very lucky. I've located a vein of coal!" He couldn't keep the triumph out of his voice.

"Oh, Worth! How wonderful! I'm so glad for you!"

"Well, yes, and thank you kindly, miss. I sure do appreciate your interest in my good fortune. But to continue with the letter. Please put in that I'm taking up my claim of one hundred and sixty acres—ought to prove far more valuable than any farm land hereabouts. And I'm now ready to press my suit—no pun intended—all the more insistently since if I have a wife, she can also take up one hundred and sixty acres." His tone was impish, and Abbie knew this was Worth's old, teasing way, but that underneath he was deadly serious. Yet now that he was back again she didn't want to be teased. She wanted him to take her in his arms and tell her he had missed her. She wanted to tell him how well she was doing—how fast she was paying off that note, how much nearer their wedding day was drawing—if he still wanted her. Her pen had stopped as these thoughts raced through her mind.

"You be sure to put that in, miss. This, er, friend of mine is mighty conscious of money affairs—dowries and such. She'll be pleased as Punch to know she can sign up for one hundred and sixty acres of land—good coal land—to help her husband out. And you can put in that I've got Indians working this very minute, building a cabin—"

Abbie said quietly, "I suppose you wish to get a favorable reply, sir? Well, I can tell you that it will be very difficult to rephrase your suggestion in such a way that it would win acceptance from even the most eager female

friend. I'm afraid, sir, that you have not seriously considered the feminine nature, which is repelled, rather
than attracted, by a statement so crudely put. If you
really desire a kind reply—"

"I certainly do. Well, miss, I said at the start that you
could phrase it better than I. Surely you can write it in
such a way that even the most reluctant girl will leap—"

Amusement and annoyance battled in Abbie's mind.
She dropped her lashes so that her companion could not
see the sudden mischief in her eyes.

"Well, sir," she said in a matter-of-fact tone, "one of
my most satisfied customers, a Mr. Tolley Heaton who
has me write all of his letters, was very pleased with one
I turned out for him this very day. His letter might serve
as a model for yours, sir, since you seem to need a model."

"Heaton, ha!" Worth snorted. "I'll bet he needs someone to write his letters—maybe even his name! Let's hear
what he considered convincing."

Abbie drew a sheet from the table drawer and pretended to read. She tried, somewhat unsuccessfully, to
keep the emotion out of her voice.

"How do I love thee? Let me count the ways.
I love thee to the depth and breadth and height—"

"You little fraud!" Worth stood up, drew her to her
feet and looked into her eyes.

"Abbie! Darling Abbie! What is your answer? You
know that letter was meant for you."

"I'm like any other girl, Worth—not particularly intrigued by the thought that you are 'ready to press your

suit' now that I can take up a parcel of land for you. And—" tears stung her eyelids and her lips trembled— "and I don't think it's very kind to—to throw it up to me that I have no dowry!"

"Abbie! Abbie, my darling little girl! I didn't! I didn't—" he began contritely. His arms went around her.

Neither had been conscious of the few late customers in the store, their bustle and chatter unnoticed by the two in the corner. Now a sudden stillness startled them. Abbie's eyes went wide as she saw that everyone was watching them. She jerked out of Worth's arms and sat down behind her table.

"Do you wish to finish your letter, sir?" she asked in confusion.

Worth dismissed the spectators with a short shrug. He leaned across the table and said clearly, earnestly, "Abbie, will you marry me? Tomorrow?"

Her cheeks were burning. What a way to propose! Here in front of everyone. Did he do it just to embarrass her? She shook her head.

"I can't, Worth. You know it."

He straightened, and reaching into his pocket, withdrew a coin and tossed it on the table.

"Never mind the letter!" he said shortly. "And here's the pay for your time!" He turned and strode out of the store.

Self-consciously the customers turned back to their shopping, talking more loudly than was necessary. But nothing could cover Abbie's chagrin and hurt. She got up, snatched her coat and left the store.

Outside she walked, unseeing, her face lifted to the

sea breeze, while tears bathed her cheeks. Oh, she thought, I ought to be used to his ways by now—his teasing ways. Sometimes it's fun, but not this—not asking me to marry him in front of all those people. This is something so intimate, and he makes a mockery of it! I almost think I—" she caught herself up sharply. No, she would not say she hated him. For she loved him in spite of everything.

John Carter's Indian boy Pete came into town. He stopped at the bakery to pick up some things his mistress wanted.

"How is *hyas tillicum?*" Sybil asked. She liked to use the few Indian phrases Tolley had taught them. She winked at Abbie. "You understand? You remember—*hyas tillicum* equals good friend equals Hortense."

"She sad. She say she want mamma," Pete answered.

"Abbie, I'm worried about her. Mamma should be back before the baby comes, but if Hortense is anxious —maybe she should have someone."

"I'll go," Abbie said immediately. "I'll go back with Pete, if you're not afraid to stay alone. Look—maybe Hortense isn't feeling too well, and there may be a lot of things I can do. I may stay overnight—so why don't you have Mrs. Parker stay here with you, if I don't get back?"

"Abbie, you're the best ever! If you will go out I'll be so relieved. And you'll stay with me tonight, won't you?" she asked the buxom woman who was helping her in the bakery.

"To be sure, Sybil. I wouldn't dream of letting you stay here, right in the center of town, alone at night!"

Sybil giggled. "I'd be safe enough, I'm sure."

"Well, then!" Abbie said decidedly, "I'll pick up a few things and be off. I think we'll all feel better if we find out what's what. If Hortense is sad and wants her mother it may be that she's nearer her time than we think."

At the cottage Abbie found both Hortense and John cheerful and busy.

"Oh, that Pete!" Hortense said with a laugh when Abbie told her what the boy had said. "Well, of course, I did say to John that I hoped Mamma would get back before the baby comes. But as for being sad—well, no one could be happier than I am!"

"I'll stay tonight, anyway, if you wish," Abbie offered. "There must be things I can do."

"Indeed there are! You can hem diapers for one thing," Hortense agreed. She brought out a stack of flour sacks, carefully washed and bleached. John moved chairs out into the autumn sunshine, and the two women sat sewing and enjoying the warmth.

"I love it out here," Abbie remarked. "So quiet and peaceful. Compared with Boston, Seattle is a restful place. And compared to Seattle, this is paradise!"

Hortense smiled. "We like it. Only when I think the baby might come when I am alone, I get a bit scared."

"Dr. Maynard will make it, no matter what. You just have to send Pete for him. You don't expect the baby right away, do you?"

"I don't know," Hortense answered slowly. "I sort of thought, even before Mamma left, that the time was getting short. But I didn't say anything. I wanted Mamma to have a little rest—a little time to enjoy her new life—

well, yes, a honeymoon. Then last night I got a bit frightened, but I didn't want to scare John—and nothing happened, after all. Maybe tomorrow I'll go into town, or else have you send Dr. Maynard out here when you go back."

The next morning John left early with two of his workers to go out to Meigs's mill for lumber to finish the sheds he was building against the winter storms. He took his wife in his arms and studied her face with anxious eyes.

"Will you be all right, darling? I won't be gone long —should be back early this afternoon. I won't go if you think—"

Hortense patted his cheek comfortingly. "I'll be all right. Abbie will stay with me, and there's Pete. If I need the doctor—"

"If I thought you would, nothing could drag me away!" John declared.

"Oh, John! You are more scared about this than I am! Go along, dear, and don't worry."

But after her husband had left, Hortense's pretense of assurance gave way. Abbie stared anxiously at the pale, distressed face.

"Do you want me to send Pete for Dr. Maynard?" she asked.

Hortense wiped perspiration from her brow. "I don't know, Abbie. I don't want to drag him out here for nothing. I did that once, you know, about a week ago."

"Well, you just lie down and relax. I'll do the dishes and straighten things up," Abbie said cheerfully. She helped Hortense over to the big bed with its pretty pieced coverlet. A paroxysm of pain brought the perspiration to her forehead.

"Abbie!" she gasped, "you'd better send Pete. I just don't dare wait any longer."

Abbie called the Indian and gave him instructions. "Hurry!" she urged, then she went to work doing the dishes, putting the room to rights. From time to time she cast a worried glance toward Hortense who lay uncomplaining, though at times Abbie could see she was suffering severely. After an hour had passed, Hortense spoke quietly.

"Listen, Abbie. Dr. Maynard gave us some instructions—he always does when folks live out of town. I think I can tell you what to do. The first thing is to put a kettle of water on to boil."

Abbie was relieved to have something more to do. She filled the copper kettle and set it on the little ship's stove, cramming wood under it to make a roaring fire.

"At the hospital," Hortense asked, "did you ever help with a birth?"

"No. No babies were born in the hospital except for a couple whose mothers needed special care. Catherine helped the doctor with those. I did get things ready, and took care of the babies afterward. But don't worry, Hortense, please! Dr. Maynard said I was a natural-born nurse. Now we'll see whether he was right."

She helped Hortense get undressed and into bed. "I'll make you some tea," she said, eager to keep busy.

Hortense gulped down the strong liquid. "How long does it take, Abbie?" she asked again and again.

Midday came, but neither felt like eating. Hortense was really suffering now, and Abbie was worried. She tried to recall everything she had heard about what to do. She went to the door and looked for Pete. Why was he taking so long? Why didn't John come?

Hortense groaned. How hard it was, Abbie thought. How very hard. What was it the Bible said? "In pain shalt thou bring forth children"? But the pain passed and the child remained, a comfort and a joy. She thought of the close companionship of Mrs. Wright and Sybil; of Dan Phillips' pride in his inquisitive Tommy; of the Widow Corey and her darling Chrissie and loyal Jeff. She must keep her mind on the children.

And then, suddenly, Hortense gave a sharp cry of intense pain. Abbie ran to her. She had heard that cry before. The baby was coming! Frantically she tried to remember everything Dr. Maynard had ever said about what was done in such cases. Finally the baby was born.

"It's a boy!" she said.

Hortense smiled weakly. "John will be glad."

Abbie wrapped a bit of linen about her finger and very carefully swabbed out the tiny mouth. Then she rubbed the baby's body with the white lard Hortense had saved in a jar for this purpose. She wrapped the baby in a blanket and laid it aside, and went to take care of Hortense.

It was soon all over. The baby lay soft and tiny beside his mother. Hortense's eyelids drooped, and Abbie felt like crying with relief. She walked slowly to the window and there were the two canoes—John's and Pete's. John and Dr. Maynard were running up the path, the worried husband somewhat ahead of the older, heavier doctor. He burst into the room.

Abbie held up a silencing hand. "Shh! I think—"

But John was beside the bed, on his knees, and had gathered his wife into his arms.

"Darling! Darling! Are you all right?"

Hortense smiled. "Look at our son, dear! Isn't he beautiful?"

John gazed at the small, pink face. Then he rose and turned away to hide the tears of relief and pride that filled his eyes.

Dr. Maynard was in the room now. He nodded to Abbie, but wasted no words. He went to the bed and made a swift, careful examination of mother and baby. Then he chuckled.

"I've said all along, Abbie, child! You are a born nurse. No one could have done more or better!"

# 12

ABBIE THOROUGHLY ENJOYED THE NEXT
two days. Caring for the tiny baby, keeping house for her
friends, nursing Hortense filled every minute with pleasant activity. From her bed, the young mother watched
the girl as she went about her tasks, humming softly.

"Dr. Maynard may be right," Hortense observed, smiling, "when he says you're a natural-born nurse. But I
think you're a born housewife and mother!"

Abbie was holding little Horace. She bent to rub her
cheek against his fluff of hair. "I've almost come to that
conclusion myself," she said softly.

She laid the baby beside his mother and went to the
stove, where a kettle of soup was bubbling merrily. "The
folks should be here any minute now," she said. Then
added slowly, "I almost hate to have them come! I've
loved every minute here, even when I was scared."

She glanced out of the window. Tolley Heaton's
brightly painted canoe was stopping in front of the cottage, his passengers looking up toward the house. Tolley
leaped out and beached the slender craft, then turned
and lifted Sybil to the strand. They were both laughing,
and they stood looking at each other with a directness

149

and meaning that could not be mistaken. Dell Cushing was assisting his bride. Abbie turned from the window.

"They're here," she said.

A moment later Sybil burst into the room. "Where is he? Where's my nephew?" she cried. She ran to the bed and bent to kiss her sister. "I've been mad, waiting! If I only could have left the bakery!"

Hortense smiled up at her sister. "Our little Horace is in his basket there!"

She didn't need to point. Sybil had already caught sight of the clothesbasket with its soft blankets. She went to it and gently lifted the covering. "Oh!" she breathed, "he's adorable! May I pick him up?"

"Be careful, though!" her mother cried, coming in at that moment, followed by her husband and Tolley. "That girl! She's been dying to see the baby. Oh, Hortense, my dear!" She went to the bed and bent over her daughter. "Why did you let me go away? To think that you were here alone—"

"Not alone, Mamma. Abbie took wonderful care of me."

"So Dr. Maynard said." She turned to Abbie. "And I'll never be able to tell you how grateful I am, my child. Here, Sybil, let me take him!"

"Let me show him to Tolley, Mamma. Look, isn't he beautiful?"

Tolley wasn't looking at the baby. He was staring at the picture Sybil made, standing there, aglow, with the baby in her arms. "Well—" he muttered.

Hortense laughed. "He'll improve, Tolley. Just you wait and see!"

Sybil relinquished the child to his grandmother, who carried him triumphantly to her husband. "Well, my dear, we're grandparents! What do you think of that?"

John came in and there was noise and chatter all around. Abbie went to the stove and stirred the soup.

"I suppose you are all hungry," she said. "I'll have lunch on the table in a minute."

Sybil ran to her and gave her a quick hug. "Abbie, you're a darling! But I'm envious that you were here and I wasn't. I'll help you with the lunch."

"I'm glad you came," Abbie fibbed quickly. "Now I can get back to my desk and the work that's piled up. Not that I've minded my little holiday. It was fun, really."

"That's why we had Tolley bring us. We thought you'd want to go back to town. Mamma and Dell and I are going to stay, though. We just must get to know the baby!"

On the way home, Abbie sat studying her companion. "Tolley, why do you keep on squiring me around?" she asked.

Tolley, surprised, was inarticulate for a moment, then he said, "Well, I sort of always thought we'd get married someday, if you ever changed your mind. Or when you got Mercer paid off."

"Why?"

"Ah, you know why, Miss Abbie. I picked you out that first day—"

"You don't love me, Tolley."

He flushed. "What makes you think that?"

"Lots of things. That 'Miss Abbie.' If you loved me you wouldn't call me 'miss.' "

"Aw!" he was obviously flustered. "It's just a habit I got into—"

"But you don't really love me, do you?"

He brought miserable eyes to face her squarely. "I thought I did. I honestly thought I did!"

"But now you know better. Let's call it quits, Tolley. It isn't fair to either of us to keep on going places together, acting as if we were planning someday to stand together before a minister—"

"Do you love somebody else, M—Abbie? Worth Barton?"

"Yes," Abbie answered honestly. "I love Worth. If I marry anyone, it will be Worth. And you—you love Sybil Wright. So you ought to start courting her, Tolley."

Tolley was really embarrassed now. "How did you know?" he mumbled.

Abbie laughed. "Oh, Tolley! Did you think you were hiding it? Why, every look you give her, every tone of your voice when you speak to her, the way you and she laugh and joke together—I've been suspecting it for some time, but today I knew for certain."

"But I don't reckon she cares for me."

"Yes she does. You ask her and see. But from now on, you ask Sybil, not me, to go to the parties and lectures and to church with you." She leaned forward and touched his arm with a gentle gesture. "It will be better, believe me. It's no use pretending about a thing like this."

"But what will you do? I still think you're the prettiest,

sweetest girl. I wouldn't want to make things hard for you."

"Don't worry about me. I'll be all right—far better, I'm sure, than if we drift along as we have been doing."

The look of puzzlement in his dark eyes could not hide the relief he felt. "Well," he said at last with a sigh, "if that's the way you really want it."

"That's the way I really want it," she said firmly.

Back at the store Abbie found that there actually was work waiting for her. Les Crismon was sprawled in the client's chair. He had been her steadiest customer ever since the day she sewed the button on his shirt. Every time he was in town he had a letter for her to write, though she sometimes doubted that there was a recipient at the fantastic addresses he suggested. He was waiting for her, idly sketching on a sheet of paper. Henry Yesler, one of the most important men in the town, was standing by the desk, twiddling his thumbs impatiently.

"I wuz here first," Crismon said, "but you go on and wait on Mr. Yesler. He's a lot more important than I am, and I reckon a lot busier."

"Thank you," Yesler said briefly. "It won't take me long. Miss Cabot, I want twenty copies of this letter made." He laid a scrawled sheet in front of her. "Here's the list of names I want to send it to. Can you get them done by tomorrow noon? I could pick them up then."

Abbie glanced over the original and nodded. "Yes, sir. I'll have them ready. You just want me to write the letter and enclose it in envelopes addressed to this list. You'll mail them yourself?"

"That's correct. I'll be in tomorrow, then."

Abbie laid Yesler's letter to one side. "And now, Mr. Crismon, can I help you?"

He held out the sheet he'd been working on. "Yep. You can write my letter on this here piece of paper. I sort of decorated it up a bit, as you can see."

Abbie glanced casually at the paper and a surprised, delighted chuckle broke from her.

"Why, that's very, very good! Mayn't I have it?"

The lumberjack flushed with pleasure. "Why, yes, miss. Of course, if you really want it."

"Oh, I do! It's exactly like me!" She held it before her, smiling with appreciation. Dan Phillips stepped over to look at what was pleasing her so.

It was just a quick pencil sketch of Abbie sitting at her table, the tip of the penholder between her lips, her head bent thoughtfully. It was the pose she always assumed when she was really thinking. Her hair in little curls on her brow, the frown of concentration, the heavily lashed lids lowered toward the paper before her—all spoke eloquently of pretty concentration. It was very lifelike and amusing.

"Why, Les!" the store owner exclaimed. "I didn't know you were an artist. You can draw that good, you can make me a picture of my little girl. It's her ma's birthday and she'd sure appreciate a picture of Rosie Belle."

Crismon was flattered and flustered. "Soon's Miss Abbie finishes the letter for me," he promised.

Others in the store drew around. The attention made the lumberjack nervous. He stuttered and stammered as

he tried to tell Abbie what to put in the letter. At last he
gave up.

"Let it go, miss! I'll figure it out and come in again.
Where's your kid, Dan? I'll get to work on that."

Dan went out back and brought in his three-year-old
daughter. He set her up on the counter and Les went to
work.

The customers crowded around, watching. Abbie
smiled to see them. They were all so avid for any sort of
diversion.

Amos Brown, one of the owners of the Seattle Hotel,
stepped close to Abbie.

"Listen, Miss Cabot. I came in to have you write an
advertisement for me to put in the San Francisco paper.
D'you think Les, there, could draw a picture of me and
my partners in front of the hotel? I'd pay him, of course.
I'd like the newspaper folks to put it in their window
along with the ad that goes in the paper."

"I'll ask him," Abbie promised.

Arthur Denny fished in his pocket and drew out a
folded sheet. "Here's that poem you wrote for me to give
my wife, Miss Abbie. Get Les to draw a bunch of violets
on it, will you? Mary's fond of violets."

So, easily, without her wish or direction, Abbie found
she had a partner and that the nature of her work had
subtly changed. Instead of writing only personal letters
to folk in the States, or simple verses for some local occasion, she was now kept busy all day long and often
well into the night, turning out every type of writing
needed by the settlers.

Les Crismon put in hard days felling trees for Meigs's lumber mill. But when his work was done he washed up and changed. Then he canoed the fourteen miles to the Seattle dock and spent his evenings in Phillips' store, illustrating poems and letters.

As the Christmas season drew near, Abbie's work increased and the money rolled in. During the six months since the arrival of the *Maria* she had managed to pay a little more than half of her note. But the drive to get it all paid had rather petered out. Ever since she had held Hortense's baby she had known in her heart that if Worth asked her again she would say yes, whether the note was paid or not. For that day, holding the small, warm body, she had known that pride and stubbornness were poor substitutes for a home, a husband and a child.

But since it didn't seem likely that Worth would ask her again, she would go on and pay Mercer. She should have her debt wiped out by spring—by May, surely. And then—then she would go to Worth.

Madame Damnable came into the store, her double chin quivering with rage, her fat, beringed hands fluttering. She sailed up to Abbie.

"I got a job for you, miss, for you and that fellow that draws the pictures. I want you to write a poem about me and my lodginghouse, and a picture of me on it. I've already thought of the first two lines and you can go on from there. But it's got to be nice— You got to brag me up better than you did the Seattle Hotel! Humph! That rat over there—three rats! They put a big notice in the papers that their hotel was the best place to stay in this town. A lie! A barefaced lie. But I'll do them one better.

I'm going to send my poem with my picture to every news-paper on the Pacific Coast from Vancouver to Mazatlán. And to every ship's office and every hotel. You take my word, miss, anyone who even thinks of coming to Seattle will know about Madame Damnable's Lodginghouse."

Abbie tried to calm the woman down. "Won't you sit down, please, and tell me exactly what you want?"

"I want sheets of good paper, about so big." She held her hands out, some six inches apart. "I want that fellow to draw a good picture of me at the top. And you write the poem underneath. I've thought how I want it to start:

> I don't want to brag or tattle
> But when you're in Seattle—

What do you think of that, miss? That'll tell them, won't it? You go on from there and say what a good place I have. Something like—

> Don't stay with any rat or louse
> But go to Madame Damnable's Lodginghouse.

Say! That's not bad, is it? Maybe you'd better use that."

"About how many of these do you want?"

"I want a hundred! And if you do a good job of it I'll pay you a hundred dollars. But I want them quick, so's they can go out on the *Eliza Anderson* next week."

Abbie gasped. "A hundred! I don't know whether Les can do the drawing on so many in that time. He works all day, you know."

"A hundred dollars if you get them done—"

"You don't have the paper you want, do you?" The woman shook her head. "Well, that will cost and take time, too. I don't know—"

It was a tremendous amount of money for one week's work, even though two of them would be sharing it. But it was a big job—writing out a hundred so-called poems in ink. And the drawings. Could Les possibly do a hundred decent copies in a week of evenings?

"I'll have to ask Mr. Crismon," she said.

Madame Damnable spluttered a little but finally left with one last injunction. "You get the best paper in town and do a good job. I'll be around next Tuesday before noon to pick them up!"

Crismon was willing to do the job. "Shucks, I can do a hundred pictures of old Ma Damnable easy as falling off a log. She's not very handsome, though, and I don't think it'll be very entertaining work. But for one hundred cart wheels I'd do most anything!"

"I'll have to buy the paper—and envelopes," she said.
"We'll take that out when she pays us."

It wasn't easy to find a hundred sheets of good paper in the town, but by hunting in the various stores she managed finally. She had to purchase new pens and ink. Altogether she put out one dollar and forty-three cents.

"That's not bad!" she told Sybil's mother. "Next week I'll have more than fifty dollars to pay Mercer, what with the work I've already done." She sighed. "It's a funny thing, but I'm not nearly so set on paying off that note as I was six months ago."

The woman looked at her. "You're not becoming discouraged about Worth, are you?"

"It's not that. But when I was out at Hortense's John said something that set me thinking. He said men feel as if they can do so little for their womenfolks. Maybe we—maybe I ought to be a bit less determined—"

Mrs. Cushing smiled thoughtfully. "That was very penetrating of John. But it's true, dear. I've always thought that is why men like to be the boss, the protector, the giver of gifts. Oh, they'd hate to admit it, but I think it sort of soothes their feelings—makes them think they are, well, repaying us for bearing their children."

Abbie said, "I'd never thought of it that way." She smiled suddenly. "My, I'll warrant they'd be surprised if they thought we'd found them out!"

Mrs. Cushing chuckled. "Well, I long ago discovered that it doesn't do a mite of harm to let a man think he's doing you a favor—whether you want that favor or not."

Abbie and Les worked every night, and by Tuesday morning the verses were all neatly written, the drawings of Madame Damnable all completed. Abbie carried them carefully to the store and waited with impatience for the woman to come and pick them up. She came in finally, her purple silk dress rustling, the crimson ruffles making her florid face look even rosier.

"Did you get the job done, miss?"

"Oh, yes, indeed. Here they are!" Abbie held out the top sheet for the woman's examination. She read it over, frowned and read it again.

"It's not very good," she said at last. "You don't say anything very fancy about me! Didn't use what I told you to—"

"Oh, yes, I did, Madame Damnable! The first two lines. See!"

"But the next two—about the rat and the louse—they're not here. They were pretty good. When I told the fellows over at the house they laughed fit to be tied! Why didn't you put them in?"

Abbie felt like saying, "Because they were horrible! The first two lines were horrible! The whole job was horrible! That's why!" But she'd counted on that money; she and Les had put in their time. She said carefully, "I didn't think they were quite genteel enough to represent your lovely house. You maintain such a high-toned place, Madame Damnable. I just felt those lines were a tiny bit, well, not quite up to your usual aristocratic style."

The woman beamed; her double chin palpitated with pleasure.

"I suppose you are right, miss. Well, I'll take them and thank you for getting them done." She gathered up the sheaf of verses and turned away.

"Madame!" Abbie said quickly, "are you forgetting? That is one hundred dollars."

The woman whirled on her. "A hundred dollars!" she screeched. "For this little pile of measly letters? These horrible drawings? And not even what I told you to put in? I declare you must be mad!"

Abbie stared. She could not believe her ears. "But you said yourself—you offered—I'd never have done that big job in such a short time if you hadn't—"

"You are mad, I do declare! You certainly misunderstood me. However, I intend to pay you, of course! A fair amount. I don't have the money just now. I'll bring it in one of these days. Good-by, miss!" And she swept out of the door.

Abbie was shocked beyond speech. She turned miserable eyes to the store owner.

"Dan! Did you hear that!"

He nodded. "Yes, Miss Abbie. I heard. I didn't know you were doing a job for her without pay in advance or I'd have warned you. She'll never bring in the money, you can be mighty sure of that. We've all learned our lesson. I'm sorry I didn't know what you were doing, what she had let you in for."

"Oh, well!" Abbie said with a deep sigh. "I'm out nearly a dollar and a half in hard cash—and about twenty hours of tiresome work! I don't know what Les will think —what he was counting on his share of the money for. But me—I'd hoped to have one tremendously good week!"

# 13 ◄◄◄◄◄◄◄◄◄◄◄◄◄◄◄◄◄◄◄◄◄◄◄◄◄◄◄◄◄◄◄◄◄

CARL NORDSTROM, THE HANDSOME, BLOND
second mate on the *Eliza Anderson* came into the store.
He was clutching a sheaf of white envelopes. He dropped
into the client's chair and leaned across the table toward
Abbie.

"What's happened between you and Tolley Heaton?"
he asked directly.

"Nothing, really," Abbie answered. "Why?"

"How is it he's Sybil's beau now? Why is he taking her
places instead of you?"

"Because he wants to, Carl. Isn't that reason enough?"

"I suppose so," he answered slowly. "But every time
there's been a shindig when the *Eliza* was in port, I've
taken Sybil and Heaton's taken you. Now all of a sudden
it's changed!"

"But there's no party going on—"

"There will be." He laid the stack of envelopes in front
of her. "Next week when the *Eliza* is here it will be Captain Finch's birthday. We officers have decided to give
him a surprise party—something very exclusive and elegant. These are the invitations. But before I distributed
them, I wanted to make sure I'd have the partner I
wanted."

162

Abbie laughed cheerfully. "And Sybil told you she wanted to go with Tolley. Oh, well, Carl, you can find plenty of girls who will be happy to have you squire them. I suppose you are not aware," she teased, "that you are the most charming officer on the ship and a great favorite with everyone."

"Well," he agreed complacently, "none of us seems to have any trouble outshining the lumberjacks around here."

Abbie knew this was true. The *Eliza Anderson* made a weekly trip between San Francisco and Seattle. It had to lie over one night and sometimes half a day or more, and the officers were very popular. They were friendly and courteous and willing to do errands in the California city. Scarcely ever did the vessel tie up without dozens of parcels brought as a personal service for the women of the settlement. And, of course, if a party or dance was in progress, the young officers were on hand to enjoy it and help the girls enjoy it.

He smiled now, the blue eyes friendly in the scrubbed-looking Nordic face. "Will you go with me, then, Abbie?"

Abbie hesitated, wondering whether Worth would be in town and invited. Nordstrom went on, "It's going to be a very small party because there isn't room on the *Eliza* for a big one. We'll dine about four o'clock and then dance afterward—on the deck. We want to make it extra nice. And there'll only be twenty couples, all told —and all young and gay!"

Why not accept? It would be unthinkable to be left out of such a gala event.

"I'll be glad to be your partner, Carl."

"Very well, then—"

Abbie was amused. "It will be the same foursome, only a different combination."

"You won't be embarrassed going with me? With Tolley and Sybil along?" the officer asked worriedly.

"Of course not! We're all friends."

Nordstrom shuffled through the envelopes before him. "Here's your invitation, then! I'll come around about half-past three next Tuesday. And thanks, Abbie! It's going to be one humdinger of a party!"

After he left, Abbie opened the envelope. The invitation was very elegant, professionally engraved. She had never before received such an aristocratic missive. Suddenly she thought of her clothes. It would be too cold, even in the afternoon for her dimity, and her bombazine was out of the question. Oh, she should have refused! In all the months she had been here she had hoarded every penny to pay Mercer. She hadn't bought anything but serviceable, everyday material for dresses to wear in the store. Some of the girls had money of their own, like Annie Mercer. And some had brought pretty things with them. They'd all wear their very best and most would probably have new dresses, maybe brought up from San Francisco. Of course, she thought sadly, Sybil's pink muslin would not be appropriate, but she would wear it with such an air that folks would think she had a dozen at home and chose the pink because she wanted to.

Driven by these thoughts, Abbie rose and went across the store to the shelves where there were bolts of material.

She couldn't afford a new dress, of course, but she could look and wish.

She scanned the shelves. There were bolts of dull brown herringbone and gray twill and blue worsted. Then her eyes lighted on some pale blue cashmere. She touched it. It would make up beautifully. And there was a pretty lavender jacquard. But I wouldn't want lavender again! she thought.

Eliza Phillips came and stood beside her. "You thinking of buying stuff for a dress?"

"No. I was just looking—"

"If you were," the woman went on slyly, "you'd best not buy it from the bolt. Too many others buy the same stuff and in a small place like this, it isn't much fun to see your dress sitting around the wall at every social."

Abbie smiled, her fingers lingering on the blue cashmere. "But what else can one do?"

"You can ask me if I don't have something special hid away. Sometimes we get just enough for one dress—if it's extra nice. Come here, I'll show you, since we're alone just now."

She went behind the counter, stooped down and drew out a long box. Abbie watched curiously. In all her days in the store she had had little time to observe the techniques of the owners.

"Just look here, Abbie!" Mrs. Phillips opened the box. She took out some packages, loosely wrapped in thin paper, and laid them on the counter. When she folded back the wrappings Abbie gasped. Here was the stuff for a queen's wardrobe.

Almost reverently Abbie's fingers caressed the material

—pale blue silk with a woven fleur-de-lis in gold thread; a stiff black taffeta that she knew would almost "stand alone," a golden merino, soft as a baby's cheek. Then she saw the one piece that made her mouth water—a moss green velvet. She lifted up one fold of the material and watched the golden glint where the light struck it, the mellow shadows in the drifted folds. She leaned to it and sniffed.

"It even smells good!" she whispered. "New cloth has such an enticing fragrance. I'm sick of the odor of old stuff!"

"You'd look mighty nice in that, Abbie. Or this!" Mrs. Phillips displayed a wine-red brocade. It shimmered in the sunlight that came diffused through the dusty windows.

"Yes, that's beautiful, but it's not for me. That's what Sybil would like—and how lovely she would look in it!" Her fingers still caressed the moss green velvet. "How much is this?" she asked timidly.

"Well, it did come all the way from Italy to New York and then down around the Horn and up to San Francisco. And it's thirty-four inches wide. Fourteen yards there are —enough to make up any style—"

"I know. So it must be awfully expensive—"

"Yes, it is. But it's worth every penny. I'd have to get eight dollars for the piece, Abbie."

Eight dollars! But oh, it was lovely! If Madame Damnable had only paid her she'd be tempted. Scarcely knowing what she did she asked, "And the wine brocade?"

"It's seven dollars and thirty-five cents. Abbie, why

don't you buy a piece? You'd not have to pay me right now. I'd trust you."

"No. I've never bought what I couldn't pay for." She stood there feeling the velvet, smelling it, feasting her eyes on its luscious color and texture. Suddenly she whirled and went across to her table. She took her tin cigar box out of the drawer and opened it. Dimes and half dollars, quarters and dollar pieces lay in a silvery heap. With feverish fingers she began to count the coins. Thirteen dollars and twenty cents!

She stared down at the money. It was Mercer's really. She wouldn't think of getting the velvet for herself unless she could get the brocade for Sybil. She had never been able to make a spontaneous, generous gesture to show her love for this friend. Never!

"Oh, I'm sick of thinking of Asa Mercer! I'm sick of waiting—of wanting!" She picked up the box and marched over to where Mrs. Phillips waited, confident that she had made a sale.

"If you'll trust me for two dollars and fifteen cents," she said boldly, "I'll take both the velvet and the brocade!"

Afterward she could not imagine what had possessed her. The bundles lay on one end of her table and every time she glanced toward them her heart stood still. She had spent money that really belonged to someone else for something she didn't actually need.

"But I do need it!" she said to herself. "I need something to cheer me up after my disappointment over Madame Damnable's job! I am not going to regret it!"

She went home carefully carrying the two big bundles. Sybil was in the room behind the shop that served as living room, dining room and work room. Besides this, the house boasted a tiny kitchen and the original small bedroom which was shared by the two girls. Dell Cushing had built on a larger room for himself and his wife.

"So you are going to the party on the *Eliza Anderson?*" Abbie began gaily. "It's to be something more elegant than Seattle has ever seen, Carl tells me."

"Yes," Sybil answered cheerfully. "I'll look like a rose in November in my pink muslin, but I'll dance hard enough to keep warm!"

"Why not wear your new wine-red brocade?" Abbie asked. She tossed the bundle down in front of Sybil.

Mystified, Sybil picked it up and opened it, and the gorgeous material leaped out in a glowing cascade that shimmered in the candlelight. Sybil just stared.

"Where on earth?" she gasped finally.

"From Phillips' store. Where else?" Abbie forced her voice to sound casual. "I thought you'd look marvelous in that. As for myself, well, I chose something a little more modest."

She undid her own package and flung a length of the velvet across the silk.

"Abbie! Abbie! Abbie!" was all Sybil could manage.

Her mother came from the shop to find out what was causing the commotion. She stood petrified at the sight of the material.

"I just decided it was time for Sybil and me to have new dresses," Abbie explained. "But now we'll have to work like beavers to get them made in time for the party next week. Oh, but won't we be the belles of the ball, though!"

Sybil ran to her friend, flung her arms about her and gave her a delighted hug. "You shouldn't have done it, Abbie! I know you shouldn't! But I'm glad you did. Oh, let's find some of those *Godey's Lady's Books* and pick out a style. Mamma! Mamma! you'll help us make them?"

"Of course I will, child. It will be a joy to work on such beautiful stuff." She turned to Abbie and there were tears in her eyes. "You are a dear child, Abbie. We won't try to thank you!"

It was worth discarding her lifelong habit of careful thrift, Abbie decided, as the two girls surveyed each other when they were dressed and ready for the party. Sybil's brocade had been fashioned into a dress with a snugly fitting bodice, shirred sleeves and a draped skirt beneath which peeped a pleated taffeta ruffle. Abbie had chosen a high-waisted style for her moss green velvet. It was simply trimmed with strips of the velvet, braided to form an edging that was sewed down the front and in loops above the hem to simulate an overskirt. From the low-cut bodice, her neck and shoulders rose, firm and creamy. Her hair, softly curling, was held by a band of the braided velvet fastened with a gold brooch.

Tolley looked at her with admiration. "You're still the prettiest girl I ever did see!" he said. Then, confused, he turned to Sybil. "You don't mind me saying that?"

"Of course not!" Sybil said, laughing. "She's always been beautiful, but tonight—well, she's just superb!"

A warm flush crept up over Abbie's neck and face. "Don't tease!" she begged. But she knew they were right.

She was beautiful tonight. If only it was for Worth instead of Carl Nordstrom.

The party was all that the gallant officers of the *Eliza Anderson* could have desired. Under a golden afternoon sun, long tables were arranged on the deck and loaded with wonderful things to eat and drink—foods Abbie had never before seen, brought from all corners of the world: lobster and oysters, artichokes and pineapples, anchovies and caviar and *pâté de foie gras,* Danish pastries and Scotch shortbread and French fruits glacé. The lucky two score young people who had received invitations nibbled at this and that, enjoying the sight and smell of the exotic foods as much as—and sometimes even more than—the taste.

When the dinner was over, the tables were removed and George Frye's Seattle Brass Band, hired for the occasion, struck up a lively dance tune. It was a polka, Abbie's favorite, and Carl Nordstrom swung her out onto the deck, where they hopped, pointed their toes, and swung gaily to the merry tune. As they danced the officer sang softly,

> "Have you seen my,
> Have you seen my,
> Have you seen my new shoes,
> With the bows on,
> With the bows on,
> With the bows on the toes!"

As the dance ended in a gale of laughter, they became aware of a commotion on the other side of the vessel. Carl drew Abbie's hand through the crook of his arm, and with his fingers still upon her hand, led her toward the gathering crowd.

"Let's see what's going on," he said. Smiling, Abbie went with him.

A file of dusky Indians, each bearing a heavily loaded sack on his shoulders, was coming up the gangplank. Leading them was a white man, dressed like his companions, his dark hair bound by a soiled headcloth. Under the sack he carried, his face and body were grimy. Abbie stared. It was Worth!

He came onto the deck, dropped his heavy burden and straightened up. Only then did he become aware of the gaily dressed group watching him. For a moment his eyes traveled over them till they came to Abbie, still held close to Carl Nordstrom's side. Their eyes met for a moment. Then Worth's slid away, with no sign of recognition. But Abbie knew he had seen her. Suddenly she pulled her hand from the officer's arm.

"Where's Captain Finch?" Worth asked curtly. "I must see him."

The Captain came forward. "Look, fellow! I'm busy right now. If you wish to see me, come back tomorrow morning."

Worth's voice was courteous but determined. "I'm sorry to have come at an inopportune time, sir. But I must talk to you tonight. My men here have come a long way bearing heavy loads. They cannot be asked to carry them farther while we search for a place to stay overnight. What I have to say will take only a moment—I want to sell you this coal—I'm sure it's the best coal you have ever used; probably the best in the world."

Captain Finch frowned. "I can't buy your coal sight unseen—" he began.

"Then let me give you a demonstration. It will take only a few moments. In your own furnace, sir! You can see what my coal will do."

"Oh, let's!" someone cried. "Oh, Captain Finch, let's see what happens!"

Pretty Inez Denny clasped her hands about the officer's arm and smiled up into his face. "I've never seen your engine room, Captain Finch, nor those stokers with their muscley arms shoveling coal. It will be such a lark, sir!"

Captain Finch grinned down at his companion. "If you'd enjoy it, my dear! Perhaps," he looked at his guests, "you young folks will excuse us a few moments. I can't let you all go down into the engine room at once, you know! But Miss Denny, here, and—" He looked at the eager group, every one of whom waited expectantly, "Officer Glenn!"

The first mate stepped forward. "Yes, sir!"

"You and your partner, Miss Manning, may come if you wish. I'm sorry," he apologized again, "but we can't all crowd below. So please go on with your dancing. We'll not be long, I promise! Come along, sir!" He nodded curtly to Worth, who picked up his sack of coal and followed the chattering quartet down the companionway.

Abbie turned to Sybil. "It's Worth! With coal—real coal, I guess. He must be working his mine."

Sybil nodded. "I know! Why didn't you speak to him, Abbie?"

"He didn't seem to want to be recognized," Abbie said slowly. Then, "Oh, I do hope Captain Finch likes the stuff! If Worth can mine coal, the ships will be his best market, I'm sure. And he will have done what he came here to do, which is more than I can say for myself!" she ended a little bitterly.

The band swung into a schottische and Tolley claimed her for the dance.

For the next half or three quarters of an hour Abbie was kept busy. She could not forget that Worth was below, having his fate settled, but there was nothing she could do. So she danced and laughed with the others under the bright Chinese lanterns that lighted the deck.

She had just finished a galop with Phil Strang, who had escorted Grace Loring to the party. Flushed and breathless, she leaned against the ship's rail and lifted her face to the evening breeze. Her glance fell on the smoke-stack, which was gleaming red against the dark sky.

"Look!" she exclaimed, startled. "It looks as if the smokestack is red hot!"

Carl Nordstrom's eyes followed her gaze. "It is! It's red hot! Oh, my heavens!" He dashed away from them and went leaping down the companionway.

A moment later an excited group came chattering up onto the deck. Captain Finch stared at the glowing smoke-stack and then flung around toward Worth, his face florid with anger.

"You! You fool!" he shouted. "You and that damned coal of yours! You'll have the ship afire in a moment. Nordstrom, get below and have that fire doused!"

Worth was grinning. "I told you it was good coal," he said happily. "So much more efficient than that Chilean coal you use now. That's half slag. This is all coal!"

"Good! You fool! It's too damned good! Excuse me, ladies. But I am upset. Don't you know our furnaces aren't built to handle stuff like that? Half slag, eh? Well, that's good enough to boil water and give us steam. That stuff you have is dangerous. Get it off my ship!"

The grin left Worth's face. "You can't mean that, sir! Why, with my coal you can get all the steam you want with half the fuel you use now. Think of the saving in money and in cargo space. The only trouble tonight is your men threw on too much—"

"Silence, sir! There's nothing to be said. Get that damned stuff—pardon me, ladies—off my ship at once!"

Worth shrugged, his face grim. He motioned to the Indians to pick up their sacks of coal, and strode toward the gangway. Abbie ran after him.

"Worth! Worth! Wait a minute!"

He strode on. Abbie lifted her skirt in both hands and sailed down the slanting, cleated planks. On the dock she caught up with him.

"Oh, Worth! Don't listen to him! Other ships will want your coal, bigger ships with more intelligent captains."

He turned toward her. The colored lanterns swinging above the deck cast a muted glow onto the dock, but it was light enough for him to see that Abbie was beautifully gowned. He reached out and touched the soft velvet. His voice was cold.

"Even if they do, which tonight looks doubtful, it will be a long time before I could buy you a dress like that."

"I bought it, myself!" Abbie cried, hurt. "And made

it myself! Worth, why are you angry at me? I have faith in your coal."

"Then we have one thing in common, but that seems to be about all!"

"Will I see you tomorrow, Worth? I want to!" she added earnestly.

"I'm afraid I'll be busy, and you'll probably be tired after dancing all night with officers who have nothing to do in port but be gallant to the girls! I had no idea," he went on bitterly, "that Mercer went to all his trouble to provide dancing partners for the officers of the *Eliza Anderson.*"

Abbie knew now what was wrong. He was angry at her for being with Carl Nordstrom. And his anger was intensified by his chagrin at appearing in his soiled work clothes before all the dressed up young people of the town. He liked to look disreputable, but in a sort of elegant, nonchalant way; not grimy like this.

"You are angry and disappointed, Worth!" Abbie said, trying to keep the tears out of her voice. "But you have no right to be disagreeable with me."

"And no right to be agreeable, either, it seems. But here comes your partner, impatient at being left alone five minutes." He turned on his heel, spoke to the waiting Indians and disappeared into the darkness.

Carl Nordstrom came leaping down the gangway. "Abbie! Everything's under control. Come on, it's another polka. We mustn't miss it!"

Abbie took the proffered arm and turned back toward the ship. But even the lively music, the brisk steps, the laughing companions could not lighten her heart.

# 14 ◄◄◄◄◄◄◄◄◄◄◄◄◄◄◄◄◄◄◄◄◄◄◄◄◄◄◄◄◄◄

ABBIE CAME THROUGH THE BAKERY SHOP
and into the big room behind it. Her cheeks were rosy
from the frosty winter air. She stopped inside the door
and sniffed deeply.

"It's beginning to smell like Christmas!" she declared.

Dell Cushing, enveloped in one of his wife's big calico
coveralls, looked up from the batter he was stirring.

"It ought to, child! All the spices in this here batter
for the Christmas cake!"

"Ouch!" Sybil gave a little cry as the hairpin with which
she was poking out walnut meats stuck her finger.

Abbie laid down her bundles. "Well, I'll help. Let me
seed the raisins, Mrs. Cushing. I'm an expert at that."

"And what in goodness' name are all those packages, if
it's not snoopy to ask?" Sybil said curiously.

Tying an apron around her slim waist, Abbie sat down
beside her friend. "I've gone into the toy business," she
explained. And when everyone turned to look at her, she
went on, "Well, I was making something there in the
store when I had nothing else to do—a little stuffed
animal for the baby. And Arthur Denny came in and saw
it and wanted to buy it. So I promised to make him one.

Then Dr. Maynard asked me if I'd have time to make something special for Catherine, and of course I couldn't refuse. And pretty soon, there I was with a stack of orders. I'll have to work every evening till midnight, I guess. But there are so few toys in the town and so few pretty things for the men to give their wives and sweethearts! Well, that's it! I'm in the Christmas gift business, willy-nilly!"

"Sounds mighty Christmasy to me!" Mrs. Cushing said, beaming. "My, how we used to send our needles flying, making aprons and doilies and pin cushions and such for everyone we knew."

"But Abbie!" Sybil said doubtfully. "Did they buy the stuff—"

"No, but they'll pay for the gifts. Sybil, it's going to mean quite a little windfall for me—for us—if you'll help me with the things."

"Of course! I need money, too, even if I don't owe Asa Mercer!" Sybil answered. "Oh, Abbie, it will be fun."

"I'll lend a hand, too, when I can," Mrs. Cushing said. "But what with the holiday orders and the seventy-eight gingerbread men for the children's party, I may not be able to do much."

Every morning after this, Abbie took half a dozen or more items to the store with her—toys, bibs, aprons, satin-covered boxes and other knickknacks. She arranged them on her table and happily watched them being picked up by eager shoppers.

She loved the store at this season. The usual somewhat musty odor of leather and jute, tobacco and apples, rubber and sawdust and sweaty people was now spiced and sharpened. Crates of oranges and lemons, wooden pails filled with striped peppermint sticks or bright red cinnamon balls, jars of pungent horehound and long strips of licorice candy all added their enticing fragrances. On the counter, large jars filled with sugary orange and citron and lemon peel invited both sight and taste. Tin canisters of ginger and cinnamon sticks and nutmegs spiced the air. Every time one of these was opened to fill a customer's order, Abbie breathed in the aroma of far, exotic lands.

And the sounds of Christmas! The cheery greetings, the laughter, the children's voices shrill with delight, filled her heart with a strange yearning to hear just one other voice, one other laugh, one other cry of wonder. Whenever she permitted herself to think of Worth, she felt that she could not bear Christmas without him, though she would probably have to. She had heard no word from him since that unhappy night of the *Eliza Anderson* party.

She knew she should be happier than she was. The tin cigar box, fed by the sales of her handiwork, was growing heavier and heavier. She could make a substantial payment to Mercer this month.

When she took the money to him she was surprised to find that he had not expected her to pay anything at this holiday season.

"Do you really want to give me this now, Miss Abbie?" he asked. "I thought, perhaps, you'd be needing extra money for Christmas—presents and clothes and things. If this will run you too close, maybe you'd better wait till after the holidays."

"Oh, thank you, sir!" Abbie cried. "That's very kind of you. But I've done well this month, and maybe you, too, need money for Christmas."

The big party for the children was to be held on
Christmas Eve, so that the day itself could be devoted to
the religious observance of Christ's birth. The event was
geared to childish interests, the adults to draw their
pleasure from watching the youngsters. There would be
a program, games, refreshments, and at the very last a tree
and a Santa Claus to distribute gingerbread men, candy
and gifts to every child in the settlement.

On the morning of the big event, Abbie did not go to
the store at all. Hortense came early to help her mother
in the bakery, so that Sybil could go with the other young
folks to decorate the hall.

Sybil dropped to her knees beside the clothesbasket in
which little Horace lay.

"Oh, he gets more adorable every day! I wish I could
just stay here and play with him all day!"

Hortense beamed. "He sleeps most of the time, so
you'd just be wasting your talents."

"Let us hold him a few minutes, anyway," Abbie
begged.

"Of course," the young mother agreed. "But you two
are going to spoil him. Never did a small boy have such
adoring aunts!"

They left at last, their arms loaded with paper chains,
cornucopias, and strings of popcorn and cranberries.

Abbie buried her face in the cranberries. "This is the
smell of a New England Christmas! I'm so glad they grow
here in Washington Territory just as they do back East.
I think I could enjoy a Christmas lacking everything but
cranberries!"

And Worth! she added to herself, surveying the noisy

group in the hall. What kind of Christmas was he having out there in the forest, alone with his Indians? If she only knew how to find him, she would be tempted to go to him, carrying a Christmas dinner as a peace offering.

When the hall was decorated and the tree trimmed, the women brought hot coffee and doughnuts for the workers. Then they all went home to dress for the afternoon affair.

"We must do honor to the children!" Abbie said, smiling.

And they do honor to us! she thought later as she looked over the rows of eager faces.

"They actually do shine, Sybil!" she observed. "As if Christmas candles had been lighted inside them."

Abbie stood crowded in with the other adults behind the benches reserved for the honored guests. The curtain was drawn on the stage to hide the tree until the dramatic moment when it should be revealed in all its glory. But in front of the curtain there was room for the child performers to stand while they sang the songs or recited the "pieces" their mammas had so painstakingly taught them.

Tommy Phillips was on the stage mumbling, "The Night Before Christmas," when Abbie felt the curls at the nape of her neck stir. It felt exactly as if someone had blown lightly across her neck. But that was ridiculous! The curls stirred again. Abbie turned, annoyed. Worth was standing there, smiling down at her, his eyes filled with the old mischief. He took her arm.

"I don't see any of your beaux hanging around you," he whispered loudly enough to be heard by those nearest her.

"Shhhh!" Abbie cautioned. Her heart was dancing.

Worth had come. Her Christmas was complete. And she was glad! glad that he was still the old Worth, teasing and annoying.

"I'm sure glad there's a little room near you for me to crowd in!" he whispered again, hissing noisily, so that their neighbors could not help hearing.

"Shhhh!" Abbie begged.

He tugged at her arm. "Let's get out of here! I want to talk to you. I want you to listen to me and not to that kid up there!"

As he manipulated her through the crowd toward the door, Abbie's thoughts were racing. Don't, don't quarrel with him again! she cautioned herself. It's not bearable— the sleepless nights, the anxious days, the worrying. I love him. Why not be honest about it? Why not yield a little— be kind and generous? If he asks me again to marry him, I'll say yes, she thought, throttling the memory of her note to Mercer and her own deep wish to settle it.

Outside the early December night had fallen. The air was clear and cold, the purple sky star-studded. They strolled down the short path from the hall to the beach. The tide was out, and below the gray rocks along the shore, the sand was hard and cold. They found a smooth flat rock and sat down. Worth's arms went around her.

"Oh, my love!" he said gently. "I've been such a fool! Such a stubborn, lonely fool, nursing my jealousy, trying to make myself believe that you did not care, just because you did not sit and mope when I was absent. Darling, can you forgive me? Can you forget my childishness and say you'll marry me?"

Abbie raised her face to receive his kiss. "I'll marry you tomorrow if you wish!"

For a moment Worth was absolutely still, as if he were letting her words seep into his consciousness. Then he said slowly, "You have paid off your note already? Why didn't you send me word, or come to me? You knew I was waiting!"

"No. I haven't paid it all. I'm on the last hundred, now—and I could get it paid in a few more months. But—" She was silent for a while. Then she turned to face him. "Worth, don't men sometimes give their wives a wedding present?"

"Of course they do. I've already picked out what I want to give you."

"Well . . ." The words came slowly, with difficulty. Surrender wasn't easy. "You can give me that note, if you want to. I am yours, darling, my debt and all!"

He kissed her then with an ardor he had never before shown. There was passion and joy and relief and triumph in that kiss. His lips found tears on her cheek.

"You're crying, sweetheart! Why?"

"Because I'm so happy."

He held her close and rested his cheek on her hair, where her shawl had fallen back to leave the soft curls uncovered. They sat there, quiet, savoring their happiness.

At last Worth said earnestly. "I'd like to give you what you ask, my darling. I've wanted to for months. But there's a better present than that. Let me give you, instead, the few more months you need to pay Mercer yourself. I love you and I know you so well!" he kissed the top of

her head. "I know that in that determined little heart of
yours there would always be a shadow—maybe faint, but
a shadow, nevertheless. A feeling of failure. The note
itself is just a symbol, of course. But I don't want you to
come to me humbled and defeated. I want you to come as
you always have, head high, independence flying! Let me
give you a few months of time, my darling!"

Now the tears came freely. "Thank you, Worth, thank
you so very much."

When their lips met there was perfect peace and understanding in their kiss.

At breakfast the next morning Dell Cushing regarded
the two girls with shrewd interest.

"Look at them, Nellie! Appears those Christmas stars
last night got caught in their eyes!"

The girls looked down at their plates, trying to hide
their telltale happiness. But the corners of their lips
curled upward. Slyly they raised their lashes to peek at
each other.

"Sybil!"

"Abbie! You, too?"

They broke into a gale of laughter.

"Now what's all this?" Nellie Cushing asked, coming
in from the kitchen with a plate of fragrant crullers.
"Share with me!"

Sybil jumped up and ran to her mother. She flung her
arms about her, giving her a quick hug.

"Mamma! Mamma, I was going to tell you! Tolley's
asked me to marry him. Right away! Oh, Mamma, I'm so
happy!"

Her mother set the plate on the table and looked at her daughter.

"Are you sure, dear? Are you sure that's what you want?"

"Oh, yes, Mamma! That's what I want more than anything!"

"But," her mother hesitated, "I thought—only a few months ago you were saying you loved Roger Conant."

Sybil smiled ruefully. "I did love Rod, in a special way. He was so much fun to be with. But Rod's a boy compared to Tolley. He could never have lived here and been happy. Tolley's a man—my man!" she ended simply.

"He's a mighty fine man, too," Dell put in. "He'll make her a fine husband."

"Oh, thank you, Dell!" Sybil cried. "Mamma, we want to get married right away—maybe on New Year's Day."

"So soon? But what about clothes and things for a wedding? We won't have time—"

"White would be nice, but then I have my red brocade! Nothing could be nicer for a winter wedding! And I'll have time to make other things for the house after I'm married. Oh, Mamma, say it's all right!"

Her mother drew her close and kissed her. "Of course it's all right, darling, if that's truly what you want."

Dell looked across at Abbie. "Is it to be a double wedding, child?"

Abbie shook her head. "No. Worth and I are not getting married until spring."

Sybil put her arms around her friend. "I don't see how you can wait!"

"I wonder at it, too!" Abbie said, her eyes serious.

Because there were so many activities going on during the week between Christmas and New Year's Day, Sybil and Tolley decided to have a very quiet wedding, with only the immediate family present. Tolley, like so many of the young men in the Territory, had come there alone. His family was in Louisiana, and there wasn't time even to get word to them.

On New Year's morning the Reverend Daniel Bagley was again called upon to officiate at the marriage of another of Mercer's party. After the quiet ceremony there was a gala dinner at the Cushings' and then Sybil kissed her mother and sister, baby Horace and Abbie good-by. With her little chest loaded into Tolley's canoe, the couple set off for the cabin he had built near Meigs's mill.

Worth had stayed on to attend Sybil's wedding. His arm drew Abbie close.

"This marriage fever certainly is contagious!" he whispered.

"You've said that before," Abbie agreed, "and today I'm inclined to agree with you."

"Well, there's a cure—" Worth began. Abbie waited. Then, relaxed, he went on soberly. "It won't be long, darling. And I'll see you often. I'm going to work that vein of coal for all it's worth, but I'll come into town every week. You can count on that."

And I have so much to do, Abbie thought. I must get that note paid off.

By April it was done, but it had been a close call and had taken every penny Abbie had earned since Christmas. After the holidays her income had dropped sharply.

There had not been so many letters to write and no sale for toys, but she had managed, by helping at the hospital whenever she was needed.

Abbie and Worth thought they would like to have a quiet wedding like Sybil's, but Mrs. Cushing would not hear of it.

"It wouldn't be fair, child. We haven't had a real big shindig for months! And you have so many friends from your work in the hospital and at the store. No, you must have a real wedding."

Les Crismon organized a committee to decorate Yesler's Pavilion for the event. The new, open-air structure had just been completed, and this would be the first celebration in it. Dr. Maynard headed the entertainment committee and hired George Frye's Brass Band to play for the wedding ball. Eliza Phillips took over the preparations for the outdoor barbecue which would precede the dance.

Abbie surveyed her meager wardrobe. It was too warm for the moss green velvet, the only good new dress she had been able to afford. Well, she'd just have to settle for the lilac-sprigged dimity for her wedding dress. She washed and starched and ironed it, hoping no one would remember how many times it had been worn.

She was busy stitching new velvet bows in place among the ruffles when she heard the familiar whistle of the *Eliza Anderson*. She had sent invitations to all the officers, and she thought pridefully, Now let Captain Finch see my successful owner of a prosperous coal mine! Other ships had been glad to purchase the coal that Worth's Indians carried to town in a steady stream.

She was still working on the dress when she heard Worth's light step. A moment later he was in the room. He dropped the parcel he was carrying, took her in his arms and swung her around.

"Why are you in here slaving when it's your very last day of freedom? After tomorrow, you'll see how I keep your nose to the grindstone. And it's such a beautiful day. You ought to be outside, dancing, with roses in your hair!"

"Oh, Worth, you never change! Set me down. I have so much to do. Maybe a man can dance on the grass the day before his wedding, but a girl is busy."

Worth set her down and picked up the sprigged dimity. "My favorite dress! I'm going to have it framed, as I told you." He tucked it under his arm and made as if to carry it away.

"Worth! Don't! I've got to finish it—"

"Oh, so this is to be your wedding gown? Tch! Tch! I sort of expected my wife to have a new dress for such a special occasion!"

Abbie's laughter died. "I know. But—" her voice faltered.

Worth kissed the trembling lips and his voice was gentle. "Don't explain, my darling! Here's something that just arrived on the *Eliza*. Maybe it will sort of make up for my wicked teasing."

He picked up the parcel, unwrapped it and spread out before Abbie's amazed eyes the most beautiful wedding gown she had ever seen. White lace and mull cascaded in rich, full flounces from a tight-fitting bodice of creamy satin. Abbie stared at it, enraptured.

"Do you like it, Abbie? I had to leave it up to Carl Nordstrom's judgment, but Nellie Cushing assured me that he was used to shopping for the ladies of Seattle." The old teasing note crept back into his voice. "He said he knew your size—he's held you in his arms often enough—"

"Just dancing!" Abbie said defensively. Then her face crumpled and she hid it against his breast. "I can't help crying. It's so beautiful! I never hoped—I never dreamed of owning anything like this!"

Almost reverently, she lifted the gown from its tissue wrappings. She called Mrs. Cushing to come and see. Hortense came, too, carrying fat little Horace, now almost too large for his mother's arms. The two women were almost as deeply stirred as Abbie at the sight of such loveliness.

"You'll be the most beautiful bride Seattle has ever seen!" Hortense declared.

Because of Worth's religious preference, Abbie had decided not to have the Reverend Daniel Bagley perform the ceremony, though he had officiated at so many of the rites for Mercer's passengers. Instead, they would be married by the Reverend David Hyland, in the new little Gothic chapel of the Trinity Episcopal Church on Third and Jefferson streets. It was to be a traditional wedding, with Dell Cushing giving the bride away, Sybil as her attendant and Tolley Heaton as best man.

The church was filled to overflowing. As Abbie came down the beribboned aisle on the arm of Dell Cushing, and saw the friendly faces turned toward her, she could scarcely bear the emotion that flooded her whole being. There was but one shadow—the wish that her own beloved father were the one walking beside her, and that her mother could be there.

In front of the altar, Worth came to her side and she saw that all the teasing and laughter were gone from his eyes. He wore a handsome well-cut suit, its narrow trousers, tight waistcoat and form-fitting jacket setting off his strong, lean body. He was carefully shaved, and his thick, curling hair was cut to lie snugly in front of his ears. A little fear tightened Abbie's throat. This was a New York man, a man of wealth and refinement, not the careless, happy-go-lucky fellow who had teased her and laughed at her for the past year and more!

But at the reception in the pavilion that afternoon, Worth was his old self again—laughing, teasing, dancing with an abandon that swept his partners, breathless, off their feet. As he released Abbie after the first set, he whispered, "Farewell, my sweet! I'm afraid I won't get another dance with you until the band starts playing 'Home, Sweet Home'!"

Abbie looked up adoringly. "I'll hate every minute of it, seeing you out there on the floor with those idolizing females in your arms."

At last the familiar strains of the last tune came across the floor. Men hastened to claim their partners. Worth came to Abbie. His eyes were tender as he took her in his arms for this last dance of their wedding night.

The next morning their possessions were packed into canoes and taken up the Dwamish to where the Black River entered the larger stream, then up the Black River to Worth's homestead. Abbie had never been so deep in the virgin forest around the settlement. Here and there they passed narrow footpaths that came to the river's edge. They saw small groups of the Dwamish brush shelters; caught sight of bronze bodies, half-clothed, watching them from the sheltering trees.

The canoe was beached on a low, sloping, grassy bank, where a group of curious Dwamish waited to greet their *Klootchman*, the bride of their patron and friend.

*"Kla-ha-ya!"* they chanted. Broad smiles brightened the dark faces as they looked upon the pretty, friendly newcomer. *"Kla-ha-ya!"*

Abbie had learned enough Chinook to understand them. She answered, smiling, "Thank you! Potlatch tonight! Big potlatch!" Then to Worth, "You were planning to give them a party, weren't you? I'm sure they expect it."

"Of course. It's all been arranged."

Abbie and Worth ascended the gentle slope and suddenly before her eyes was her home, a luxurious log cabin nestled among towering trees. The sun, slanting through the boughs, struck real glass windows, making them gleam invitingly. At each end of the building was a huge stone chimney for the two fireplaces inside.

But what caught at Abbie's heart was the sweetbrier rose, twining up around the door posts and over the lintel, bright with the dainty pink flowers that had come to mean "Seattle" to her.

"However did you do it?" she asked wonderingly. "It looks as if it had been growing there for years."

"I told it you were coming, my sweet, and it broke into blossom."

"But how, really?"

He would tell her someday how carefully he had transplanted and trained that rose for her sake. But not now.

He picked her up and carried her across the threshold. Inside the big, bright room he set her down.

"Will it do, my sweet?"

Her eyes went about the room, taking in every detail in a swift glance: the real plank floor, not just dirt, covered with bright Indian mats; the walls hung with other mats, like tapestries; the Indian baskets filled with wild flowers on hearth and table and in the deep-set window sills. The huge fireplaces and the handmade furniture—

"A sewing machine!" she gasped suddenly. "It looks like—"

"It is! I bought it at Mercer's auction of his goods in San Francisco—for you, my darling!"

"You knew, even then—"

"Long before then! Abbie, didn't you know, too?"

"Yes," she whispered. "I knew, too!"